"What will happen to him?"

Desperate, the sheriff turned to Caleb. "Doctor?"

Caleb pointed at himself. "Me? You want me to take him?"

"In a roundabout way, yes."

Caleb spread his hands. "I have no place to keep a baby."

Rebecca looked at both men. "Why couldn't they stay with us? We have plenty of room at the ranch."

The lawman's expt work. You and Reb on an emergency b squawk too much s physician's supervis

"I—" Clearly flustered, Caleb spluttered. "I wasn't planning to stay in Burr Oak much longer."

"There's no one else to take the little guy," the sheriff prodded. "And it would only be a temporary thing. No more than a week, I'm sure."

Looking from one to the other, a sigh slipped past Caleb's lips. "Okay. I guess I can hang around until you can make other arrangements."

Rebecca struggled to keep her composure. "Are you saying we can take him?"

The sheriff grinned broadly. "You can…"

Pamela Desmond Wright grew up in a small, dusty Texas town. Like the Amish, Pamela is a fan of the simple life. Her childhood includes memories of the olden days: old-fashioned oil lamps, cooking over an authentic wood-burning stove and making popcorn over a crackling fire at her grandparents' cabin. The authentic log cabin Pamela grew up playing in was donated to the Muleshoe Heritage Center in Muleshoe, Texas, where it is on public display.

Books by Pamela Desmond Wright

Love Inspired

The Cowboy's Amish Haven
Finding Her Amish Home
The Amish Bachelor's Bride
Bonding over the Amish Baby

Visit the Author Profile page at LoveInspired.com.

Bonding over the Amish Baby

Pamela Desmond Wright

LOVE INSPIRED
INSPIRATIONAL ROMANCE

LOVE INSPIRED®
INSPIRATIONAL ROMANCE

Recycling programs
for this product may
not exist in your area.

ISBN-13: 978-1-335-59697-0

Bonding over the Amish Baby

Love Inspired
22 Adelaide St. West, 41st Floor
Toronto, Ontario M5H 4E3, Canada
www.LoveInspired.com

Printed in U.S.A.

And we know that all things work together for good to them that love God, to them who are the called according to his purpose.
—*Romans* 8:28

This book is dedicated to my readers.
Thank you all from the bottom of my heart
for making my dream come true. I am humbled
to be able to share my stories with you.

A shoutout also goes to
my fabulous editor, Melissa Endlich,
and my agent, Tamela Hancock Murray.
These two ladies were the ones who made it
all happen behind the scenes. They are both
a blessing. I am honored they have chosen to
take this journey with me.

Chapter One

Rebecca Schroder tightened her grip on the reins guiding her horse as a large vehicle sped past her buggy. As he zipped by, the driver swerved dangerously close on the narrow two-lane strip. Frightened by the revving engine, the startled mare whinnied, shifting from a slow walk to a spirited gallop. The wheels clattered.

Stomach twisting, her heart thudded. The clip-clopping of iron shoes striking asphalt echoed in her ears. Close to panic, she swallowed past the icy fingers squeezing her throat. If she lost control, the horse could veer off the road, galloping into a ditch.

Fearful of overturning, she pulled back hard. "Bebe, mind yourself!" The mare slowed.

Pulse returning to normal, she huffed. *Englisch* drivers were so careless. Instead of minding the safety of slower-moving farm and ranch vehicles, drivers often roared by without thinking.

Ach, why are people in such a hurry?

Content to continue at a slower pace, she readjusted her bonnet to cut off the sun. Now that noon was at hand, the orb was rising into the center of the sky. Up at dawn, her entire morning had disappeared in the blink of an eye.

Horse calmed, Rebecca set her gaze toward the sprawling ranch in the distance. The land purchased by her *grossdaadi* had been in her *familie* for generations. The acreage was grazing land for cattle, specifically Texas Longhorns. Famous for the massive span of their horns and ornery nature, the bovines were in high demand. Pasture grazed on the nutritious wild grasses covering the plains, the meat they produced was all-natural and organic.

Moisture rimmed her eyes. It was a *gut* way of life. But she wouldn't be staying much longer. In another two weeks, she'd be moving into town.

Closing one door, the Lord had opened another, leading her down a fresh path. Her broken engagement to Noel Yoast had left her without many prospects to support herself. Having resigned from her teaching position, she'd turned an eye toward babysitting. She'd already decided to rent the old *dawdy haus* belonging to Elva Schrock's elderly *eltern*. He'd recently passed away and the place was sitting empty. Renovated and updated with propane appliances, the location made it perfect for the home daycare she planned to open.

It wasn't the way she'd envisioned her life unfolding. But it was a satisfactory solution to her dilemma. Her hard work in the wake of heartbreak was paying off.

"'Ask, and it shall be given you; seek and ye shall find,'" she murmured, quoting a favorite passage. She felt at peace with her decision to walk her path without an *ehmann*. She might not be a married woman, but someday she would have *youngies* to care for.

I'm getting there, Lord. Just have patience.

She snapped the reins with a practiced hand. "Giddyup."

Releasing a snort, the mare shifted into a brisk trot. A mile disappeared then another.

Rounding a steep curve, Rebecca gasped in horror. A wreck loomed ahead.

"Whoa, Bebe! Whoa!" The mare whinnied in disapproval but obeyed. The buggy rolled to a stop on the side of the road.

Rebecca pulled the handbrake, abandoned her seat and jumped to the ground. Breaking into a run, she headed toward the stunned driver. She recognized the SUV as the same one that had passed her at a dangerous speed. Though the highway looked straight, the gently sloping landscape was a deceptive one. Twisty curves often appeared out of nowhere—a danger to drivers who weren't familiar with the area.

By the look of things, the driver had abruptly swerved off the asphalt and into the gravel lining the side of the road. Skid marks indicated the vehicle had plunged through a shallow ditch before going straight through several feet of fencing. Traveling at a high speed, the SUV had taken out at least half a dozen heavy wooden posts. Tangled in barbed wire, the hood was crumpled in.

Cell in hand, a man stood near the edge of the road. Dressed in casual slacks and loafers, he wore his white shirt open at the neck and the sleeves rolled up to his elbows. Sunglasses pushed atop his head, he ruefully surveyed the wreckage.

"Are you all right?" Gaze scraping the man's tall figure, Rebecca searched for signs of injury.

He lowered his cell. "I'm fine," he said, brushing his

palm across his chest. "Wasn't expecting that bend in the road."

Relieved he was able to walk away, Rebecca cocked her head toward the nearby sign. "There is a reason the speed limit is a low one through here. You were going way too fast when you passed me a few miles back."

"Entirely my fault." He winced. "I had a lot of things on my mind, and I just wasn't paying attention. I should know better."

"We all make mistakes. Thank *Gott* only your car and some fencing were damaged."

Walking toward the wreck, the driver surveyed the mess he'd made. "Looks like I'm going to owe someone for the mess I made. And it looks like I'll need a new front end." Raising his hand, he gave his cell a shake. "I can't seem to pick up a signal."

"Cell service is spotty out here. We rely on ourselves when accidents happen."

Giving his smartphone a forlorn look, the driver tucked it into his hip pocket. "I hate to ask, but could you give me a ride into town? I need to arrange for a tow to come and pick up my car and find out who owns the fence I took down. I do have insurance, so it will be repaired."

Shading her eyes, Rebecca glanced toward the sky. The sun was a bright yellow ball of pure, unrelenting light, scorching everything beneath its unblinking eye. The heat, too, was taking on a sweltering weight. She couldn't leave the stranger stranded on the side of the road.

"Ja," she agreed with a nod. "I can take you. It's not far. Just another twelve miles."

The corners of his mouth lifted. "Thanks. I appreciate it. I apologize for the inconvenience."

"It's not a problem." Stepping forward, she offered her hand. "I'm Rebecca Schroder."

Accepting her gesture, his big hand closed around hers. His grip was firm, almost intimate. "Caleb Sutter."

Breath catching on a gasp, a ribbon of warmth swirled through Rebecca. Not only was Caleb Sutter a personable fellow, but he was also a handsome one. Tall and muscular, his tanned complexion was complemented by a mane of dark curls brushing his chiseled jawline. A few wisps curtained a portion of his brow. His nose and mouth fit perfectly between his wide cheekbones. By the wisps of silver threading his temples, he appeared to be nearing forty. His eyes were a stormy shade of gray.

Heat crept into her cheeks. It wouldn't have bothered her to stand and look at him all day.

He's Englisch. Not one of your own.

Embarrassed by her reaction, she stepped back. "Nice to meet you."

He let his hand drop. "Excuse my ignorance, but you're Amish, right?"

Rebecca glanced down at her simple clothes. With her long, knee-length dress, ankle-high black boots and heavy bonnet, no one could mistake her for anything but Amish. Travelers passing through Burr Oak for the first time were often surprised to learn that Anabaptists of the Old Order had founded the town and that a robust population of Plain folks lived there.

"Ja." She paused, clearing her throat. "I mean, yes. I am."

He cocked his head. "German, right?"

"A derivative of the *Deitsch*. Though the dialects vary by region."

"It's a nice language. Very melodic to the ear."

Her stomach fluttered again. She liked his engaging manner. *"Danke."*

Returning his attention to the damages from the wreck, he winced. "I hope the owner won't be too mad about their fencing." He shaded his eyes from the sun, and surveyed the wide-open landscape. "Don't guess you'd know their name?"

"I do. The land belongs to my *familie*." She pointed toward an unpaved county road just off the bend. "Our ranch is just down that road."

"Sorry. Destruction of property isn't the best way to introduce myself."

"You're not the first one to miss that turn. And there are no cattle grazing that land right now, so we don't have to worry about strays." Fanning a hand in front of her face, she cocked her head toward her buggy. "Come with me. I know a mechanic you can talk to."

"Sounds good. Any place I can rent a car?"

"You can rent a cargo van at U-Move-It."

"Is that the best I'm going to get?"

"Ja. They're quite popular. A lot of Amish rent them and a driver for the day."

"I suppose that will do. Once I get some wheels, I'll come back and settle on the fence."

"Levi will be fair, I'm sure. He'll want nothing more than the cost of materials."

"Sounds like a plan. I promise I'm good for it." Walking toward the buggy, he eyed the unwieldy conveyance. "I've never ridden in one."

"Just grab on and step up." Holding on to the side of the buckboard, Rebecca hefted herself onto the seat. It wasn't ladylike, but it got the job done.

Caleb copied her. His movements were clumsy, but he made the climb without falling. "Whoa, that takes some agility." Settling down beside her, his leg and elbow brushed hers.

Rebecca subtly scooted over.

Noticing her discomfort, Caleb tucked in his knees and folded his hands in his lap. "Pardon me, please. Didn't mean to crowd you."

"You're fine." Claiming the reins, she released the handbrake. "Hang on. It's a bumpy ride." Flicking the mare's rear end, she urged the horse to get moving. "Giddyup, Bebe. Let's go."

Trotting at a brisk pace, the mare headed down the road. The clattering of the wagon permitted the conversation to drift into silence.

Acutely aware of her passenger's proximity, Rebecca kept her spine straight and her eyes on the road. No one would say a word about giving an *Englischer* a ride into town. Still, there was no reason to invite folks to wag their tongues. Her breakup with Noel had already given people enough fodder to gossip about.

The sooner I drop off Caleb, the sooner he can take care of business and be on his way.

"You did a good job tearing it up," the mechanic commented behind a wry grimace. "By the look of those pictures, the entire front end is goin' to have to be replaced."

Nodding, Caleb lowered his cell. Having snapped pictures from every angle for his insurance company, he'd suspected the vehicle was in sorry shape. Approaching the curve too fast, he'd overcorrected, going off the road and straight into the breakdown lane. Instead of riding it out, he'd panicked and hit the brakes.

Sliding hard on the gravel lining the side of the road, he'd fishtailed through a shallow ditch before striking a line of heavy wooden posts strung with thick barbed wire.

He glanced around the busy shop. The property was on the shabby side, littered with vehicles in various stages of repair. Some were in so many pieces it didn't look as if they ever had a chance of being rebuilt. "Can you do the work?"

Wiping his hands on a greasy rag, the man rocked back on his heels. Balding, tanned and clad in worn coveralls, he'd put in a lot of years under the hood. "I can."

"I know it's short notice, but can you fit me in?"

The man flagged a hand toward the cars filling his shop. "Kinda on the busy side."

Standing nearby, Rebecca Schroder lifted her gaze. "I'm sure Mr. Sutter would appreciate it if you could nudge him to the front of the line, Jim."

The mechanic scratched his stubbled chin. "Suppose I could for you, Miss Rebecca. Your pop was one of my best friends. And I sure do like those tomatoes Miss Gail sends from her garden."

"The tomatoes are overloading the vines this year, so I'm sure I could manage to bring in a sack or two next time I come to town."

A wide grin lit Jim's expression. "I'd appreciate that. And some cucumbers, if you got 'em."

"Oh, we got plenty. Zucchini, too. You'll have all you can eat. I promise."

Satisfied with the deal, the mechanic nodded. "I'm sure somethin' can be arranged."

Relieved to have moved a step forward, Caleb asked, "How long does something like this take?"

A shrug rolled off the grizzled old man's shoulders. "If I were you, I'd count on a month. Maybe longer. Depends on how long it takes to get the parts."

Great. Just great.

Caleb did a few mental calculations. He'd planned to make the trip in three days.

The best-laid plans frequently go awry.

Having come to a crossroads, he mulled his options. If he rented the cargo van, he could leave later in the afternoon. Proceeding with his trip, he could arrange to have his vehicle delivered to Los Angeles once repairs were done.

It wasn't an ideal solution, but it was workable. Once he rented some new wheels, he could follow Rebecca back to her family ranch, settle on the damaged fence and be on his way.

"Sounds good. I'll pay my deductible directly, and you can file with my insurance to cover the rest," he said and sealed the deal with a handshake.

"Guess I'll send one of the boys to tow it in," Jim said. "Where'd you wreck it?"

Caleb blanked. He wasn't familiar with the area and had relied on his GPS for driving directions. "Uh, I—I'm not sure."

"It's the twisty curve off Rabbit Road, Jim. Just down from the ranch," Rebecca added helpfully.

Jim nodded knowingly. "Ain't the first time we've gone an' got a wreck out there." He sucked in on the chaw packed in his lower lip. "By the look of those pictures, you lost a bit of fencing, too."

"It probably won't be the last either," she said.

Jim tucked his greasy rag back into his hip pocket.

"Need to slow down and mind the signs," he said to no one in particular.

Caleb raised his hands. "It was entirely my fault. I had my mind on other things and wasn't paying attention."

"Praise *Gott* no one was hurt."

Feeling foolish, he nodded. As a physician who'd tended to many victims of wrecks in the ER, he should have known better. But he'd let his thoughts wander while driving. Now, he was paying the price for his inattentiveness. The two-lane highway he'd driven on was close to deserted. Aside from miles of barbed wire fencing, there wasn't much to look at except cows. Texas was cattle country. Behind barbed wire fences, the free-range bovines spread out as far as the eye could see.

A chuff pressed through his lips. The only thing he knew about cows was that they tasted good when cooked medium rare and topped with a good steak sauce. He couldn't imagine living in a cow town in the middle of nowhere, a place where he could barely get a signal on his cell.

The unexpected presence of an open horse-drawn buggy plodding down the highway had jerked him out of his thoughts. A woman wearing a bonnet sat on the buckboard, guiding the horse. Foot tapping the brake, he hit the clutch, downshifting into second. His speed dropped.

As he approached the buggy, the woman extended her arm and made a go-around gesture. The meaning was clear. If he wanted to go any faster, he'd have to pass.

Accepting her signal, Caleb hit the accelerator. The engine revved. Taking his foot off the gas, he'd smashed the clutch, upshifting even as he'd gained speed. Checking the oncoming lane, he'd sped around the slower vehicle.

Flipping on his blinker, he'd changed lanes again. Disregarding the danger of speeding on an unfamiliar highway, he'd pressed the accelerator harder. The needle on the speedometer rose.

Unfortunately, he'd failed to notice the steep bend up ahead in the highway.

"Lesson learned."

"I'll call Elias to pick up your vehicle," Jim continued. "After that, I'll take a look at the damages and get the parts ordered."

"Thank you for fitting me in. I appreciate it."

"We'll take care of it." Flagging a hand, Jim motioned toward a small office at the front of the building. "Marta will have some paperwork for you to sign. Just give her your insurance information and you can be on your way."

"Great."

Satisfied with the progress, Caleb headed into the office to sign the paperwork. The middle-aged woman behind the desk was friendly and efficient, assuring him Jim Dyette did excellent work.

Twenty minutes later, they were rolling down the street.

Rebecca glanced his way. "Feeling better?"

"Yes. Thank you. I appreciate your help. I'm sorry I tied up your day. I'm sure you had other things to do."

She shrugged. "Just heading home for lunch. I'm a little peckish, but I'll survive."

Caleb brightened. "Perhaps you'll let me treat you to a late lunch then. After I grab a rental, I'd be glad to take you to any restaurant in town." Gaze scraping her bonnet and modest clothing, he added, "If it's okay to eat with an *Englischer*, I mean. I don't mean to offend if it's not allowed."

Eyes sparking, she released a merry laugh as she guided the horse around a corner.

"Of course, we can eat lunch. There's nothing in the *Ordnung* that says we can't have *Englisch* friends and socialize with them."

Pulse quickening, Caleb's insides twisted into knots. Sitting beside such a pretty woman made him feel like a blushing schoolboy. It had been a long time since he'd hung out with a member of the opposite sex. Though her hair was concealed under her sunbonnet, the face beneath it was a striking one. Sparkling eyes ruled over a pert nose dusted with freckles. A perfect cupid's bow complemented her cherry-red lips. Hers was a mouth made for smiles and kind words. Open and accepting, she'd offered a helping hand and her friendship without hesitation.

"Anything you like, I'm paying."

She grinned. "You like Tex-Mex? I know a place that serves the best chips and salsa. Most everything is made from scratch, and it's delicious."

Caleb gave her the side-eye. "Chips and salsa, eh? Hot or mild?"

"I like medium. Just enough for some heat, but not enough to burn your mouth."

"I'm looking forward to trying it."

Settling back on the buckboard, Caleb relaxed. A good meal with a new acquaintance would help take the sting off his terrible day. He looked forward to getting to know her and hoped she wouldn't mind if he asked more questions about the Amish.

Approaching the town's center, a courthouse, post office and library were all within glancing distance, as were a couple of churches and a community center.

A farmer's market populated by individual stalls offered homegrown produce, fresh eggs and honey. A butcher shop offered locally sourced meats and cheeses. Preserving the natural landscape, an eclectic mix of shops and sidewalks had been built to include the trees and other flora. As part of the original settlement, many streets were still paved with the original cobblestone. Horses clopping up and down only added to the ambiance.

Taking in the sights, Caleb looked every which way. From what he'd seen, the tight-knit hamlet wasn't the kind of place that invited travelers to stay long. A couple of motels offered rooms, but anyone seeking an active nightlife would be sorely disappointed. He suspected the town rolled up the sidewalks at dusk.

Brow furrowing, he searched his memory for the bits and pieces of trivia he knew about the town. Now and again, he'd passed through, but had never stopped to check it out. As far as he was concerned, one little dusty Texas town looked like the next.

Reaching their destination, Rebecca stopped in front of an off-brand rental. "Will this do?"

Caleb surveyed the selection parked beneath an awning, a total of about half a dozen. Larger trucks and trailers were also available, but he didn't need anything that excessive. Most were older models but looked to be in good shape. A cargo van wasn't exactly what he wanted, but it would do in a pinch.

He jumped to the ground. "I hope these things have stereos and power steering." At least his things would fit. Emptying his apartment, he'd kept only personal items. Rather than deal with moving a truckload, he'd pared down his possessions to the essentials. His clothes, computer and a few sentimental items were all he'd kept. The rest of it? Gone. Starting over with a clean slate, he'd intended to buy new furniture and other appliances once he'd rented an apartment in Los Angeles.

"Glad it will do." Guiding the horse to a parking place out of direct sunlight, Rebecca pulled the handbrake before looping the reins around a catch near the seat. A few buggies were also parked nearby, allowing the horses to neigh back and forth.

Amused, Caleb shook his head. The town was a curious mix of past and present. Somehow the two managed to coexist.

He waited for Rebecca to join him, then they walked toward the rental office. Opening the door, Caleb welcomed the blast of arctic air, a welcome respite from the day's oppressive heat. Hours behind schedule, he hoped to transfer his belongings to the rental, grab a quick bite and then hit the road. He'd have to drive through the night to make up for the lost time.

A young blonde woman, heavily pregnant, stood behind the counter. A look of distress twisted her features. Phone clutched in one hand, she struggled to punch the numbers on the mobile handset.

"Help, please! I think my baby's coming!"

Chapter Two

Hurrying around the counter, Caleb gave the woman a quick visual check. Panting and panicked, she might have been nineteen or twenty, but no older. Her enormous belly engulfed her petite frame. Hand welded to the phone, her eyes were full of fear.

"I wasn't ready for this," she gasped. "The baby's not due for two more weeks."

"Babies have a way of deciding their own schedule," Caleb said, answering in a steady voice. "What you need to do is calm down. Focus on breathing, in and out." He gave a quick example, sucking in air and blowing it out.

The clerk nodded. "I'll try," she managed through clenched teeth before crumpling to the floor.

Caleb dropped to his knees beside her. "My name's Caleb. I'm a doctor and I can help, but I need you to answer some questions." Glancing at the tag affixed to her uniform, he added, "Can you do that for me, Mary?"

She squeezed her eyes shut. "I think so."

"How close are your contractions?" He checked her pulse and monitored her respiration. Day in and day out, he saw people at their worst: some only mildly ill or injured—and others who were soon to draw their last breath. After ten years he'd gotten used to the misery, accepting that he couldn't save every soul that came through the ER. He could only do what he'd been trained to and hope for the best.

Mary gasped as pain rippled through her. "They just started. They last about a minute and then go away. My back and stomach hurt, too."

"Good." Caleb offered a smile of reassurance. "You're definitely in labor, but you're in the early stages, so there's still time before the baby comes."

Mary clenched her eyes shut. Tears of frustration pressed through her lids. "I don't know anything about birthing babies."

Sensing the woman's distress, Rebecca joined them. Her gentle expression was one of understanding and compassion. "*Ach*, I know you're scared, but it's a natural thing for a woman to do."

Flushing red and hot, Mary cried harder. "I don't want to. I don't want to be a mother. Make it go away." She was crushed by fright, and her words turned nonsensical. Her entire body quivered harder as another contraction clawed through her. "Please, I just want this to be over."

"Tensing up will only make it worse," Rebecca advised. "Relax and do as the doctor says. Focus on your breathing."

Mary attempted to comply, huffing in and then blowing out air. Eyes puffy from crying, her skin grew redder with the fever of pain.

Admiring Rebecca's cool head and gentle touch, Caleb nodded toward the phone. "Call 911."

Rebecca gently pried the wireless receiver from Mary's rigid fingers. "I'm on it."

"We've got to get her to the hospital."

Punching in a few numbers, Rebecca shook her head. "Burr Oak doesn't have a hospital. The nearest one is a hundred miles away. It's quicker to call Sheriff Miller. His office is just a few blocks down the street. He can get us to the clinic faster than an ambulance. It's small, but Dr. Gordon has delivered plenty of babies."

Caleb gave her the signal to go ahead. "Then that's what we'll do."

Of course, he should have remembered that many remote small towns often had only rudimentary health care. Rural areas were hardest hit when it came to recruiting competent medical professionals because of the lack of funding for facilities and staff. People often died because they couldn't reach help fast enough.

The sheriff's dispatcher answered the call. "Sheriff's office. What's the emergency?"

Caleb cocked his head. The woman's clipped voice sounded tinny and faraway over the wireless receiver. *Hope the sheriff isn't tied up elsewhere.*

Rebecca got right to the point. "Hello, Della? It's Rebecca Schroder. I'm here at U-Move-It rentals. The clerk's pregnant and she's gone into labor. Can you send Evan or one of his deputies over? You can? *Gut.* Send him now. And call Dr. Gordon and tell him to get ready to deliver a *boppli*." Listening, she acknowledged what the dispatcher said before disconnecting. "Sheriff Miller's on his way," she confirmed.

Moved by another contraction, Mary screamed and clutched Caleb's hand. "The pain's getting worse," she panted between lips pulled into a grimace. "I don't think I can stand much more."

Rebecca bent closer, attempting to soothe the distressed woman. "Help is coming."

Minutes later, a tall dark-haired man dressed in a sheriff's uniform rushed through the door. "Got here as soon as I could."

Rebecca climbed to her feet. "You'd better get us to Dr. Gordon's office, double-quick."

The sheriff nodded. "I can do that." His gaze scraped over the scene, taking in every detail. "Can she walk?"

Caleb nodded. "It'll be good for her to get on her feet." He pressed his arm against Mary's back, helping her stand. "I'm going to need you to walk on your own. It'll help the pain and put the baby into position."

Mary groaned but stood upright. "It hurts so much."

Sheriff Miller offered his support. "We're going to put you in the back," he said.

Mary struggled as the two men attempted to guide her outside. "I can't just go," she cried, distressed. "My boss will fire me for leaving the office open with no one here."

Rebecca's head swiveled. "Where are the keys?" she prompted. "I'll lock the door."

Wincing, Mary tried to point. "In my purse, on a little pink ring. It's under the counter, where the computer is."

Rebecca claimed the purse and dug inside. "Got them."

"Let's go," Sheriff Miller prodded. "Della's called ahead. Dr. Gordon is expecting us."

Leading Mary to the sheriff's vehicle, the two men helped her inside.

Satisfied his patient was comfortable, Caleb climbed in. "Easy now," he prompted. "Keep your breathing steady and focus on staying calm."

Eyes widening, Mary clutched at her distended belly. "He's going to be here sooner than you think."

"Then I guess we better get going while the going's good." Slamming the door shut, Sheriff Miller slid behind the wheel. Sending a quick message to Dispatch, he activated the lights and sirens of his emergency vehicle. Leaning over, he pushed open the passenger door. "Hurry up!" he called to Rebecca.

"Coming!" Still holding the clerk's purse, Rebecca clambered inside. "I'm ready." Her sunbonnet had gone askew. Tumbling down her back, only the ties around her neck held it in place. The neat bun tucked beneath had unraveled, spilling a cascade of brown curls around her back and shoulders. "I've never been in a police car." She pulled the door shut.

Sheriff Miller glanced at her. "Hang on and enjoy the ride." Shifting gears, he pressed the accelerator. Lights and sirens flashing, he made a U-turn before speeding down the street. Startled motorists pulled over to the curb to allow him to pass unimpeded. Driving with expert precision, he managed to reach the Burr Oak Family Health Care Center in record time. Located near the edge of town, the compact redbrick building looked like any other clinic throughout the state. A few horses and buggies were parked among the cars dotting the parking lot.

"There's an emergency entrance around back," Sheriff Miller called over his shoulder. Whipping around the building, he pulled to a stop beneath a wide awning. A sliding glass door slid open, expelling a couple of female staffers pushing a gurney.

Caleb unlatched the doors and climbed out. "Her contractions are down to less than a minute apart."

"It's Mary Reese," one of the aides said. "Dr. Gordon's ready for her."

As the women assisted, Caleb lifted Mary onto the flat surface. Moaning in distress, she kept her eyes shut and her face was pale white. "It hurts so bad," she gasped through a groan. Clenching one of his hands with both of hers, her fingernails dug into his skin. "Feels like he's stuck."

"Let's go."

The women guided the gurney through the sliding glass doors with practiced ease.

Face tearstained, Mary moaned with fear. "I can't do this," she cried, shaking her head back and forth in distress. "I don't want this baby."

Unable to free his hand from her unrelenting grip, Caleb ran alongside the gurney. Glancing over his shoulder, he saw Rebecca and Sheriff Miller hurrying to catch up. Their faces were etched with concern and compassion.

An elderly man wearing black slacks, a white shirt and a long lab coat waited at the end of a narrow hallway. Reaching out, he grabbed Caleb's arm as the female aides ushered Mary into the birthing room. The doors closed, leaving him standing outside.

Dr. Gordon shot him a severe frown. "I don't believe we've met." Huffing, his nostrils flared with disapproval. "Are you the father of this child, young man?"

Caleb countered with a quick shake of his head. Based on Mary's words, he suspected no father was in the picture. Sadly, she seemed to be all alone. Her mental state also seemed to be deteriorating.

"I'm not the father—but I am a doctor." Pulling in a much-needed breath, he hurried to add, "Mary went into labor when I went to rent a van where she works."

The old man's gruff demeanor evaporated. "You're

a doctor? Wonderful!" His eyes took on an expectant sparkle. "I could use the help."

"Glad to assist." Caleb stuck out his hand for a quick shake. "I'm Caleb Sutter. I've been the lead EMS at the ER in Summerlin for the last five years."

"David Gordon," the other man returned. "I'm going to assume you've delivered a few babies in your time."

"I have."

Standing nearby, Sheriff Miller chimed in. "Sounds like he was in the right place at the right time."

Satisfied he'd cleared up the matter, Dr. Gordon launched into his patient's history. "Last time I saw Mary, the baby had gone breech. I turned the little fella and I'm hoping he stayed where he needed to be."

"Well, he's ready to be born," Caleb countered. "No matter what position the baby's in, Mary is in for a rough time."

The conversation stalled when a woman poked her head out of the birthing room. The badge she wore identified her as Karyn, and her tag identified her as a nurse practitioner.

"We need you, Doctor," she said, making an urgent motion. The look on her face was one of concern. "Now."

Lifting his glasses and rubbing the bridge of his nose, Dr. Gordon gave Caleb a meaningful look. "If you're willing, I'll show you where to wash up. *We* have a new soul to deliver."

"She doesn't want the baby."

Unsure she'd heard correctly, Rebecca blinked. "What do you mean?"

Still clad in blue scrubs, Caleb tugged off his surgical mask before leaning against the wall in the waiting room. He rubbed his red-rimmed eyes. Several long hours had passed since the clerk went into labor.

"Mary has rejected her baby," he said after a short pause to catch his breath. "She doesn't want anything to do with him."

Shocked, Rebecca pressed a hand to her mouth. She couldn't imagine how a woman who had just given birth to a new life could turn away from her precious infant.

"What happens now?" she asked.

Sitting nearby, Sheriff Miller sat up straighter. Like her, he'd waited patiently for news of the baby's arrival. "Safe haven law kicks in," he said. "As of now, the baby will be a ward of the state while the mother is sent to a facility for a mental health evaluation."

Shaken by his reply, Rebecca felt ice circle her spine. "And if Mary decides she doesn't want her *boppli*?"

"She can relinquish all parental rights and her baby will be put up for adoption." Pulling in his long legs, Sheriff Miller stood. Fishing his cell out, he offered a curt nod. "Excuse me while I get in touch with social services and see if I can make arrangements for someone to come and take the baby."

Heart pounding furiously, Rebecca watched the lawman step to a private corner to place his call.

Stunned by the drastic turn of events, she bowed her head. Through the long hours, she'd prayed unceasingly. After a moment she found the strength to raise her gaze. "Is she sure that's what she wants?"

Caleb's lips momentarily flattened. "Dr. Gordon's trying to counsel her now, but it's my opinion that she's not in any shape to listen or make a reasonable decision at this point. Mary has stated several times that she does not want the baby. She refused to hold him and asked for him to be taken away. That's not good. Right now, he's at his most vulnerable and it's the best time for mother and child to start bonding."

"My heart aches for both of them." Pausing, she asked, "Does he have a name?"

Pulling back his shoulders, Caleb rubbed the back of his neck. "No. Not yet."

The unintended blur of tears stung Rebecca's lids. How sad to be newly born and unwanted, not even given the dignity of a name. Turning her head, she daubed at her eyes. She hadn't meant to get so emotionally invested in the *boppli*'s plight, but she couldn't help it.

The purse she'd kept for Mary still sat in her lap. Faded and worn in places, the cheap pleather thing had seen better days. Beneath her company's work blazer, the clothes the girl wore were also threadbare in places. By the look of things, Mary's ends were barely meeting.

A spike of anger filled her. Why was no one in the community helping her? Maybe Mary hadn't asked because there was nowhere for her to go. The Amish helped each other when a member of the church fell ill or struggled. But the *Englisch* world wasn't always so generous.

No matter what the answer was, someone needed to find a solution.

She considered what she could do to help women who found themselves in a difficult position. The plan she'd had to open a daycare morphed into something more. Women like Mary needed a place to go where they could get the support they needed to care for their *youngies*.

An idea began to simmer…

"Would you like to see the baby?"

Thoughts interrupted, Rebecca blinked. "*Ja*. I'd like that."

"Come on."

Swiping the tips of her fingers against her eyes, Rebecca pushed herself out of the chair. Her knees were stiff from sitting. She could use a chance to stretch her legs. Trailing in his wake, she followed him down a short hall.

Turning a sharp corner, they arrived at a small nursery. Painted in a shade of off-white, the walls were decorated with scenes from a popular children's book. Aside from the beds, there were rocking chairs and a table with chairs that would allow parents and family members to visit with the new arrival. Karyn worked around a pediatric bassinet. Dressed in a cotton onesie, the newly born infant mewled.

Caleb pushed a swinging door open. "May we come in?"

Straightening, Karyn frowned. A woman in her later thirties, her hair was clipped neat and short. Pleasantly attractive, she wore no makeup. Dressed in drab scrubs, she removed her stethoscope. "I was just about to call you, Doctor."

Expression shifting to concern, Caleb hurried to the infant's bedside. "What's wrong?"

She gave a brief explanation. "I was just checking his vitals and thought I detected a murmur in his heart."

"I don't recall Dr. Gordon saying he found any problems after birth," Caleb countered, undraping the stethoscope around his neck.

Biting her lower lip, Karyn glanced over her shoulder. "Um, Doc Gordon's been having issues with his hearing," she admitted, speaking in a low voice that wouldn't carry outside the nursery. "It's something he could have missed in the delivery room."

"Ah. Got it." Caleb bent over the infant, listening to his heart.

Rebecca's blood pressure plummeted. *Oh, no!* What if something was wrong with the *boppli*? Again, she praised *Gott* that Caleb was on hand to pick up the slack.

A silent minute ticked by, then another.

Caleb straightened. "You're right. He does have a murmur."

"Is he okay?" Anxiety high, Rebecca blurted out the question.

"The baby does have a grade-two murmur," he said, confirming the diagnosis without hesitation. "Good catch, Karyn."

Karyn beamed. "Thank you."

Rebecca looked from one to the other. Neither seemed panicked. "What does that mean?"

"It's nothing worrisome." To calm her, Caleb offered a smile. "We need to keep an eye on him." Gazing into the bassinet, he rubbed the infant on the tummy to help soothe his fussy movements. Going still, the *youngie* gazed up through wide unfocused eyes.

"What causes those?"

"Heart murmurs in infants can be caused by intense physical activity. We should probably have expected it given his difficult birth. In most cases, these types vanish in time. We'll monitor his vitals for a few days, just to be safe." He looked to Karyn. "I want you to start him on an iron-fortified formula. The sooner we get him some nutrition, the better he will feel."

Karyn nodded. "I'll do that now." Moving to a feeding station stocked with supplies, she selected a formula. Satisfied with her choice, she sterilized a bottle before filling it with a few ounces of liquid.

Rebecca watched with envious eyes as Karyn placed the bottle near a rocking chair before scooping the infant out of his bassinet.

"Would you like to feed him?"

Pleased to be considered, Rebecca glanced toward Caleb. "May I?"

"I don't see why not. He could use a loving touch."

Rebecca hurried to sit. Her pulse thudded as Karyn lowered the squirming infant into her waiting arms. Freshly bathed, the *boppli* was a warm bundle of pure joy.

Taking a breath to calm her nerves, she cradled the infant. "*Ach*, he's so little." Small and delicate, he was no heavier than a bag of sugar.

"He's got some growing to do."

Karyn offered the bottle. "See if you can get some nourishment in him."

Rebecca didn't have a chance to accept it. Sheriff Miller strode into the nursery, cell in hand. His expression writhed with frustration. "I don't believe this."

"You don't look pleased, Sheriff," Caleb said.

Miller tucked his cell away. "Bad news. There's no social service worker available to pick up the baby. It looks like we're on our own."

Stunned silence filled the nursery.

Rebecca cuddled the precious bundle closer. "What will happen to him?"

Taking off his hat, the sheriff ran a hand through his thick black hair. "I don't know." He looked at Karyn. "Could you take him?"

She stepped back. "I can't, Sheriff. I've got kids of

my own at home and we're stretched to the breaking point here because we're so short-handed. All we have for help is one aide, and she's still in training."

Desperate, the sheriff turned to Caleb. "Doctor?"

Caleb pointed at himself. "Me? You want me to take him?"

Miller nodded. "In a roundabout way, yes."

Caleb spread his hands. "I'm just passing through town. I have no place to keep a baby."

Rebecca looked between the men. "Why couldn't they stay with us? We have plenty of room at the ranch."

The lawman's expression brightened. "That might work. You and Rebecca could foster the baby on an emergency basis. The state shouldn't squawk too much since he would be under a physician's supervision."

"I—" Clearly flustered, Caleb spluttered. "I wasn't planning to stay in Burr Oak much longer."

"There's no one else to take the little guy," Miller prodded. "And it would only be a temporary thing. No more than a week, I'm sure."

As he looked from one to the other, a sigh slipped past Caleb's lips. "Okay. I guess I can hang around until you can make other arrangements."

Relieved, Miller put his hat back on. "Then it's settled. As a representative of this county, I am giving you two temporary custody. I'm sure Dr. Gordon will concur."

Rebecca struggled to keep her composure. "We'll take *gut* care of him," she promised, rocking the precious bundle.

The sheriff grinned broadly. "I've no doubt about it."

Chapter Three

Rebecca bent over the bassinet. Worry slithered through her. "*Ach*, he's such a little one. Will he be all right?"

Rechecking the infant's vital signs, Caleb offered a nod of reassurance. "You can stop fretting. He's fine."

"Thank *Gott*. When you said he had a heart murmur, I was concerned it would be something terrible."

"There's a chance he won't have it long. These things usually go away on their own. I bet it'll be gone by the time he's six months old. Maybe sooner."

"I will pray it does." Relieved, she gave her eyes a rub. The last few hours were a blur of activity. Having deemed the newborn stable enough to travel, Dr. Gordon agreed the best thing to do was to send the *youngie* into a home-like environment.

Slipping off his stethoscope, Caleb tucked it back into the black satchel he'd borrowed from the clinic. "He might have had a rough start, but he's healthy."

Giving the dozing *youngie* a final nervous check, Rebecca gently stroked his downy head. The baby had been born with a mass of thick blond curls and wide blue eyes. He also had a healthy set of lungs. As they'd prepared to transport the *boppli*, an ambulance had arrived to pick up Mary. Emotionally fragile after her difficult delivery, the young mother would be admitted to a state facility for a complete health evaluation. As Caleb had explained, it wasn't uncommon for mood disorders to arise around the time of childbirth. Early intervention was a vital step toward treatment.

"I feel so terrible for his *mamm*."

"Mary is in the hands of professionals who can give her the help she needs."

"I'll be praying for her, too. She's going through so much and doesn't seem to have anyone to help."

A gentle smile curved Caleb's mouth. "I think she'd appreciate that."

His reply impressed her. Instead of scoffing at her reliance on faith, he'd encouraged it.

Given the few hours she'd known him, she realized Caleb Sutter wasn't like a lot of *Englischers* she knew, always connected with their cell phones and in a hurry. As it stood, his phone hadn't buzzed once.

Gail poked her head into the room. "Just checking to see how the *boppli* is settling in."

Rebecca motioned for her to join them. "Caleb says he is doing well."

Tiptoeing in, Gail gazed down. A petite woman with brown hair and sparkling eyes, her thickening waist indicated she'd soon be welcoming another *kind*.

"*Ach*, he reminds me of Sammy when he was born. Same little blond curls."

Rebecca couldn't help but smile. Now a precocious toddler, her nephew was the first child born into the *familie* in decades. A little over three years ago, Gail had married Levi Wyse, an Amish orphan their father had taken to foster when Levi was about fourteen. Coming of age, Levi had left the ranch to pursue his dreams of becoming a rodeo star. His reappearance after ten long years had surprised everyone. As Levi worked to straighten out the business and its finances after Samuel Schroder's death, old feelings had come back to life for both. Joining the church, Levi wed Gail shortly thereafter. A widower, Levi also had a young *sohn* from the time he lived in the *Englisch* world. Seth was the best big brother ever and doted on his younger *bruder*.

"Think Sammy will mind another *boppli* in the house?"

"I think he'll like it." Gail laid a hand on her stomach. "He's so anxious to know if I'm carrying a *boi* or a *mädchen*."

Caleb's gaze swept over her. "If the old wives' tales are right, it'll be a girl. You're carrying high."

Surprised, Gail blinked. "I never thought I'd hear that from a medical professional."

"I've delivered a lot of babies. I've found it to be true. Sometimes they will surprise you, but since everyone loves a surprise, it has never upset anyone."

"I suppose that's a *gut* way of looking at things," Gail agreed affably. "I just came to let you know dinner's almost ready. Sheriff Miller had to leave, but I do hope you'll join us, Dr. Sutter."

He drew in a deep breath. "If it tastes as good as it smells, I'm in. I haven't had a bite to eat since I left Summerlin this morning."

"I'll have it on the table shortly. Join us when you're ready."

"Thank you."

Rebecca looked to Caleb. "Would it be better for me

to stay with the *boppli* while you eat? I can have my supper here."

"Newborns sleep quite a while after they've been fed. He's got a full tummy and isn't fussing. He will be fine while you take a break." Stepping away from the bassinet, he took her elbow and guided her toward the door. "If he starts to squall, you'll know it."

Back aching and feeling ragged around the edges, Rebecca welcomed the break. From what she'd seen, Caleb had experience handling infants. His large hands cradled the newborn with ease.

She paused to look around. Formerly a storage closet on the first floor, the space had been widened and re-modeled into an extra room. There was also direct access to a bathroom that had a shower, sink and toilet so that guests would have privacy. The room Levi had occupied as a teenager also shared access to the bath-room. Expanding the old house had been necessary. Gail and Levi's *familie* was growing. With two *youngies* and another baby on the way, these rooms would soon be given to the older *kinder* as the new ones arrived. The couple planned at least half a dozen. Maybe more.

As was the custom, the eldest *sohn* kept the home-stead. Because Samuel Schroder had none, it was only right the ranch went to his oldest *tochter* — and that was Gail. To be fair, the couple paid a portion of the yearly profits to herself, Amity, and Florene. The in-come would help cover the licensing and other fees re-quired to open her future daycare.

"I'm still pinching myself that he's here." Turning, she gave the sleeping infant a final loving glance.

Leaving the newborn to his slumber, they walked into the living room. Across the wide-open space, Gail was busy at her cookstove. Levi sat at the dining table, dandling their toddler on his knee. Heavily bearded, he looked dignified and mature. Basking in his *daed*'s attention, the chubby-cheeked *boi* squealed with delight.

Amity sat near the fireplace working on a basket of sewing. Neat with an angular face, she bubbled with good-natured tenderness and empathy. Intelligent and independent, she'd started her own business from the ground up, selling homemade products such as soaps and other skin-care items. She also made potpourri mixes and had recently begun to branch into medicinal teas and other natural remedies. Her shop was growing. She'd recently begun to explore putting her business on the internet to attract more customers.

Now a husky nine-year-old, Seth sat near the fireplace. Carving knife in hand, he carefully worked on his latest creation. The pieces took him several months to finish. Waiting patiently for scraps from the supper table, his mongrel hound lay at his feet.

As Caleb had only had a moment to meet everyone after they'd arrived with the *boppli*, Rebecca quickly reintroduced her family to refresh his memory.

Amity laid aside her needlework. "I hope the little one is settling in."

Florene barely acknowledged them. Sprawled in a comfortable chair, she played a handheld video game.

"Everyone chill. It's not like we haven't had babies here before." Dressed in faded jeans, a T-shirt and tennis shoes, she looked like a typical *Englisch* girl.

Rebecca gave her youngest sister a quick frown. "Be kind, please," she admonished, unwilling to let me rude remark pass. "The *boppli* had no other place to go."

Stirring with a quick hand, Gail glanced up from the

pan of country-style gravy. A pile of pork chops filled a platter, as did golden ears of corn on the cob and freshly baked buttermilk biscuits. A large bowl of mashed potatoes and a side of collard greens waited to be served. With a house full of hungry people, she never failed to prepare three hearty meals a day.

"I agree. If you don't have anything nice to say, then don't say anything at all."

Hackles rising, Florene shot everyone a frown. "Back to the bawling late at night." She winced. "It's hard enough to sleep around here as it is."

"Then move out," Gail shot back without blinking an eye. "Everyone's had it with your complaining."

"Being on *rumspringa* doesn't give you leave to be rude," Amity added. "It'd be better if you were putting your nose into the Bible instead of those games."

Florene's expression turned pouty. "I'm allowed to have them and there's nothing you can do."

Rebecca forced herself to hold her tongue. While embracing the *Englisch* world, her youngest sibling had turned into a brat. Florene never went to church anymore and spent her time running around with her boyfriend. Everyone in the *familie* felt she was heading down the path of ruin, but there was nothing they could do except offer advice and hope the Lord grabbed her and gave her a good shake.

Pressing Sammy against his shoulder, Levi stood. "That may be true," he said in his quiet way. "But when you are under this roof, you will respect your *schwesters* and our guest. If you can't hold your tongue, I suggest you go somewhere else."

Flicking off her game, Florene flipped it aside. "Whatever."

Embarrassed, Rebecca attempted to brush off Florene's behavior. Later, she would pull the younger woman aside and offer a piece of her mind.

"Please forgive my *schwester* for her behavior. She's forgotten her manners when we have guests," she apologized, attempting to deflect Caleb's attention from the squabble.

He spread his hands. "I am truly sorry for intruding on your family."

"Not at all, Dr. Sutter. We're honored to have you," Levi countered. "You and Rebecca are doing *Gott*'s work. That *youngie* needs you both."

Gaze locking with hers, Caleb smiled. "We make a good team."

Struck by the sincerity in his words, Rebecca drew a steadying breath.

"*Ja,*" she murmured. "We do."

While it hadn't been his intention to move in with the Schroder family, Caleb had recognized the need and agreed it would be the best thing to do. It wasn't unusual for a newborn to be released from the hospital within a few hours of birth, but most were kept for observation for at least twenty-four hours.

The baby does have a heart murmur. It won't hurt to stay a few days. Just to keep an eye on him.

Truth be told, he wasn't looking forward to sitting in an empty hotel room and eating more greasy takeout. It would also be a treat to soak in the hospitality the Amish offered.

"I promise I'll stay out of the way," he said and took a step back as the women carried the food to the table. Expecting Sheriff Miller to return tomorrow, he would consult with the lawman about the expected length of his stay. Miller had promised to keep the phone lines hot and find a more permanent arrangement for the motherless infant.

"You are not in the way." Biscuits in hand, Gail placed the plate onto the middle of the table. "Our door is always open."

"This is a godly home, and all are welcome to sit at our table," Levi added.

Excited by a new face in the group, little Samuel waved his arms and squirmed.

"Gaa, down!" he cried, clutching the rag doll he held.

Levi bent, balancing the toddler on his own two feet. "Now settle down."

Happy to be set loose, Samuel clutched his toy. Releasing a string of gibberish, he toddled on wobbly legs.

"Sammy, stay out from underfoot." Gail gave her husband a look. "Levi, put him in his high chair."

"*Ja*, I will."

Determined not to be ignored, Samuel bounced and waved his doll. "Mine!"

Setting out the high chair, Levi reached for his son. "Come here, rascal."

Giggling, Samuel shifted his tiny feet into high gear.

Rebecca bent, attempting to catch her nephew. Squealing, Samuel skillfully evaded her reach.

"He's getting faster," she exclaimed. "Soon we won't be able to catch him."

Scampering across the kitchen, the little boy ran toward Caleb and held up his treasure. "Mine!"

Enjoying the child's antics, he grinned down at the little tyke. "Aw, he's a cutie."

"Sammy, behave," Levi chastised.

"He's fine." Going to one knee, Caleb accepted the doll the child wanted to show off. Dressed in a miniature version of an Amish-style shirt and coveralls and a black felt hat, the rag doll had no face. Under the brim of the hat, the blank face invited onlookers to imagine the eyes, nose and mouth.

"I haven't seen one of these before."

"The dolls are Amish," Amity chimed in. "*Englisch* tourists love them. I can't keep enough in the store."

"Ah. They are cute." He handed the toy back.

The toddler grinned. "Mine!" he exclaimed and then raced to bury himself in his mother's long skirt.

He rose. "Excuse my ignorance, but why don't they have faces?"

"*Gott* commands that we do not make graven images," Rebecca explained. "We believe that all are equal in the eyes of our Lord and only He can make men and women."

"In case you've forgotten, men and women need to eat." Gail waved everyone toward the table. "It's getting cold. Please, sit and dig in."

The family gathered around the long picnic-style table bracketed by benches, each taking their place. Regular chairs sat at each end for guests to use.

Levi indicated a chair. "Have a seat, Doc."

"Caleb. Call me Caleb, please," he said, taking the chair at the end of the table.

Setting out bowls filled to the brim, Gail laughed. "We're all anxious to hear about your and Rebecca's day. The sheriff told us a few things but had to leave before he could finish."

Pitcher in hand, Amity filled tall glasses with iced

tea and then set out a square of butter, sugar and a small dish of lemon wedges.

Rebecca slid onto the bench on Caleb's left side. Her other two sisters sat to his right. Gail and Seth settled into their places, ready to tuck into the evening meal.

Levi claimed the remaining chair, as befitting the head of the household. He cleared his throat. "I hope you don't mind, but we like to say a prayer before we eat."

"Not at all."

"Please join hands," Levi instructed.

Caleb hesitated. Would that be proper? Was he allowed to hold hands with an Amish woman?

Seeing his hesitation, Rebecca reached out. "We don't bite." Her hand slipped into his. Her grip was sure and firm. Comfortable.

Pulse quickening, Caleb's insides twisted into knots. Feeling heat rise to his face, he quickly glanced away. A long time had passed since any woman had affected him in such a physical way. Holding her hand made him feel like a blushing schoolboy.

Amity, too, offered hers. "Please."

Grateful for the distraction, Caleb grazed her with a smile. "Of course."

Bracketed between the two Amish women, he couldn't fail to see the resemblance between them. They differed only in height. Rebecca was tall and slender. Amity was petite.

Levi continued, "As our guest, it would be fitting if you would care to say grace."

Feeling as if a spotlight had been shone his way, Caleb drew back his shoulders and sat a little straighter. "Um, I'll try." Religion had never meant much in the household he grew up in.

Everyone nodded, waiting.

Unaccustomed to praying, he searched his memory for something appropriate. Reaching back to the few times he'd attended church, he said the first thing that came to mind.

"Lord, thank you for leading me to safety and allowing me a place at this table today. I'm grateful for folks who are willing to lend a hand and share their bounty with a weary stranger. Help us use this time to bond as friends. Amen."

"That's a lovely prayer." Drawing her hand away, Rebecca unfolded a napkin and spread it across her lap. Most everyone else at the table did the same. Platters and bowls were passed around, allowing each person to serve themselves.

Caleb glanced at his plate. Normally, he didn't eat a lot of meat. But there was no way he could resist the pan-fried chops, or the mashed potatoes loaded with real butter and doused with thick country-style gravy. The meal was a feast fit for a king.

Utensils in hand, everyone dug in.

Tucked in his high chair, Samuel squirmed and kicked his legs. He swung his toy, entertaining himself.

Dealing with her fussy toddler, Gail attempted to take his doll. "Now, Sammy, it's time to put it down." For his supper, she'd prepared plain mashed potatoes and small bites of unseasoned, shredded pork.

Unwilling to part with it, Samuel held it tighter. *"Nein, nein!"*

Chuckling, Levi rolled his eyes. "He's got a mind of his own."

Gail pressed out a sigh. "I can barely pry it out of his hands."

Levi grinned. "I think he's trying to tell us he'd like a little *bruder*."

Blushing, Gail pressed her palm against her protruding middle. "Dr. Sutter says he thinks I'm carrying a girl."

Taking an interest in the conversation, the older boy introduced as Seth glanced up from his plate. "A *schwester* would be neat."

Amity offered a smile. "Oh, I do hope you have a *tochter*. I'm so looking forward to making some pretty dresses with lace instead of knickers."

Florene gave her sister the side-eye. "You need your own *kinder*," she commented rudely, dipping a piece of her biscuit into the thick gravy.

Using a sharp knife to pare her corn away from the cob, Amity shook her head. "Someday, I pray. Someday."

"I'm never marrying or having kids," Florene announced, and then angled her chin. "I intend to be a modern woman."

"That's your choice," Rebecca countered. "But don't put down the rest of us for walking a more traditional path."

Forking up a piece of meat, Caleb popped it into his mouth. Giving half an ear to the family's conversation, he compared Florene's modern clothes to the traditional Amish-style clothes her sisters wore. Their simple dresses, aprons and *kapps* appealed to him.

Rebecca smiled at him. "Is it *gut*?"

Swallowing the bite, he picked up his napkin and wiped his mouth before answering. "It's the best I've eaten in a long time. Your sister is a wonderful cook."

Across the table, Gail blushed. "You're being generous, Doctor."

"Not at all. Everything is delicious."

Amity swallowed a bite of mashed potatoes then looked at him. "Sheriff Miller told us a bit about your and Rebecca's day, but you haven't said what brought you to Burr Oak."

Knowing he owed the owner of the fence a confession, he said, "It was an accident. I'm not sure if you noticed the damage yet, but I'm the one who tore up your property."

Levi guffawed with amusement. "You own the black SUV? One of the hands saw Jim's boys towing it off, but we didn't know who it belonged to. Can't tell you how many times folks have knocked down that fence then driven off."

"I'd planned to come back and make it right once I grabbed a replacement," he explained. "But Rebecca and I got sidetracked."

"When we went to rent a van, the clerk was in labor," Rebecca continued, filling everyone in on the day's happenings.

"Praise the Lord you were there," Gail said when the narrative had concluded. "How fortunate for Mary you knew what to do."

Uncomfortable with the praise, Caleb averted his gaze. "It was nothing."

"What you did saved a woman's life—and her *boppli*," Rebecca countered. "If you hadn't been there, both might have died."

"I did what I was trained to," he mumbled. "That's all."

Rebecca pinned him under a stern look. "The Lord gave you a mighty gift. He meant for you to be here today."

"More than likely it was my bad driving."

She shook her head. "You shouldn't scoff at *Gott*'s power. The Lord brought you to Burr Oak for a reason. And whether you believe it or not, He is going to show you why."

Chapter Four

"Would you care for another slice of apple pie, Doctor?"

Caleb swallowed his last bite before shaking his head. "I couldn't." Though he rarely indulged in sweets, he'd found himself unable to resist the pie Gail served for dessert. Baked perfectly brown, the flaky crust cradled crisp slices of fresh apples coated in cinnamon and sugar and baked to perfection. Scoops of home-churned vanilla ice cream added more delicious flavor. "I think I just put on ten pounds."

Claiming his empty plate, Gail whisked it away to the waiting sink. "Don't worry. You are a little on the thin side and could stand more meat on your bones."

Caleb glanced down at his lap. As observed, his slacks were a little baggy. Truth be told, he hadn't bothered to have a decent meal for quite a while. The last year had been tough on him, emotionally and physically. It was why he'd decided to pack up and leave Texas.

Determined not to let his woes interfere with the evening, he tucked away his melancholy feelings. "If I stay here much longer, I'll soon be letting my belt out a notch or two."

Catching the tail end of the conversation, Levi laughed. "Think I've gone up two pant sizes since marrying Gail." Patting his middle, he added, "Nothing beats an Amish woman's cooking."

Dishcloth in hand, Gail gave her husband a fond look. "Oh, Levi. You're still thin as a rail. And a man who works cattle from dusk to dawn deserves a *gut* meal."

Levi gave her a quick peck on the cheek. "An excellent wife is more precious than jewels," he murmured. "And you are mine."

Blushing clear to the roots of her hair, Gail dropped her gaze as she pulled away. "*Ach*, Levi. Mind your affection. We have a guest."

Caleb pretended he hadn't witnessed the intimate moment. Part of the reason he was single was because of his intense work schedule. He didn't have time to date, much less enjoy a relationship. In a moment of wild impulse, he'd resigned his position to take on a partnership in California. Joining a private practice would give him a nine-to-five routine, and time to socialize.

New life, a fresh start.

Except his fresh start had turned into a fiasco. Struggling to pick up the pieces of his shattered life, he felt like a balloon set free in a high wind. The peace of calmer skies eluded him. Eager to embrace a sense of normalcy, he secretly welcomed the opportunity to leave his problems behind for a few days.

Reaching for the cup of coffee Gail had served with dessert, Caleb sipped the smoky brew. The grinder sitting on the countertop revealed that she ground her own rich, dark roast. He wasn't sure, but he thought he detected a bit of chicory and cinnamon in the drink. An unusual blend, it was delicious. Having consumed two cups, he doubted he'd catch a wink of sleep. Along with the excitement of the day, the caffeine was sure to keep him awake late into the night.

Taking her turn at the chore, Amity worked to get the dishes done and put away. Broom in hand, Rebecca swept up the crumbs and other bits of food her nephew had scattered on the floor. Taking his younger brother in hand, Seth entertained the toddler with a series of hand-carved wooden animals. Showing the little boy each figure, Seth made the sounds associated with each. Amused, Sammy clapped his hands with glee as he tried to imitate the roar of a lion or the neigh of a horse. Only Florene declined to lend a hand, returning to her game.

As he'd never visited an Amish home, he was also curious to discover more about their way of life. From what he'd seen, the old house was an odd mix of past and present. The kitchen had a wood-burning stove and an old-fashioned icebox. Most of the light was provided by oil-burning lamps or the fire crackling in the stone hearth in the living room. The nursery, however, had battery-powered lamps, and the adjoining bathroom had modern fixtures and conveniences. Overall, the home was a cozy one, and full of love.

A pang of sadness momentarily washed over him.

He no longer had a home. Or a family.

Throat tightening, he forced himself to swallow. Now wasn't the time to have an emotional breakdown. He was supposed to be a professional who knew how to hold things together when life delivered one of its devastating curveballs.

Physician, heal thyself.

Given time, he hoped he could.

Satisfied with everyone's work, Gail clapped her

hands. "Grab your Bibles, everyone. We need to give a little time to the Lord."

Glancing at Caleb, Rebecca added, "If you aren't too tired, we would love for you to join us."

Feeling it would be rude to turn down the invitation, Caleb indicated his willingness with a nod. Raised a Christian, he'd drifted away from the church. He only attended two times a year: on Easter and Christmas Eve. Working in an ER, he saw the worst of tragedies, the desperation on people's faces as they prayed for loved ones to be healed. Often, God seemed to turn a deaf ear to their pleas. Surrounded by so much misery, he'd begun to doubt the Lord had a hand in people's lives on a day-to-day basis.

A sudden wail shattered the calm.

Rebecca's eyes widened with alarm. "The *boppli*!" Disappearing into the nursery, she returned a few minutes later with the small bundle cradled in her arms.

Everyone gathered around. Moving his head from side to side, the infant mewled, sticking out his tongue.

"*Ach*, he's letting us know he's hungry," Gail said.

Amity headed back into the kitchen. "I'll warm his bottle." She dug the infant's formula and bottles out of a travel bag.

Reluctant to get involved, Florene made a face as her sisters fussed over the baby. "He's not that cute," she said, putting her stamp on the matter.

Caleb decided it would be best to keep his distance. Though the Amish seemed somewhat backward with technology, the women were experienced when it came to childcare. The Anabaptists had managed to survive and thrive for quite a few centuries. As it was, he couldn't find a single drawback in their simple, wholesome lifestyle.

Settling onto a sofa near the fireplace, Rebecca offered the infant his bottle. "He's a *gut* eater," she commented when the baby latched on and began to nurse. Nodding toward the thick volume sitting on the end table, she looked at Caleb. "Would you mind sitting beside me and holding my Bible so I can read along during the lesson?"

Caleb rose. "Not at all." Cup in hand, he made his way into the living room. Each member of the family had a place, settling in for the night's lesson.

Claiming the Bible, he sank into the cushions of the well-worn sofa. Acutely aware of Rebecca's close presence, his pulse bumped up a notch. The effect she had on him was hard to deny. There was a definite attraction.

You're an outsider. An Englischer. *These aren't your people.*

The thought pained him. Without thinking twice, he thrust it into a dark crevasse deep inside his mind.

As she gazed at the infant, a sad expression washed across Rebecca's face.

"Something wrong?"

"He has no name. Mary never said what she wanted to call him."

"A name expresses essence," Gail said sagely. "It should reflect something about him and his birth."

Rebecca nibbled her lower lip. "We have to call him something—even if it's only temporary."

"The little fella deserves one," Levi agreed. "And I don't think anyone would mind."

All eyes turned to Caleb.

"Would it be all right to give him a name?" Rebecca asked.

"As Levi said, I don't think anyone would mind." Aware of the Bible in his hands, Caleb opened the cover and scanned for the first name he found. "Matthew sounds nice."

Rebecca's expression glowed. "Matthew," she exclaimed. "How strange the Lord should lead you to it."

"Why?"

"It means 'gift from *Gott*.'"

"Then Matthew it is," he said.

Everyone nodded, agreeing the name was a fitting one.

"I like that you went to the Bible, Doctor," Amity remarked. "Are you a religious man?"

Unsure how to answer, Caleb looked at the book he held. It was dog-eared and well marked, and Rebecca had also scribbled many notes in the margins.

"I'm not sure," he drawled. "I'd like to believe there is something more beyond this world we see, but I'm just not sure. Sometimes I wish there were a way to know for certain."

Gail cocked her head. "The miracle of birth isn't enough to convince you?"

"Ah, that's simple biology."

"It's more than biology, Doctor. It's a miracle that the love between a man and a woman can create a new soul. *Gott* gave us the ability to have *kinder* so we would know the joy he felt when he created Adam and Eve."

Caleb mulled over her reply. "When you put it that way, I guess it makes sense."

Levi leaned forward. "Would you care to know the Lord as your savior?"

Closing the thick book, Caleb ran the pads of his thumbs over the faded lettering covering its face. The question echoed through his mind.

Is this what it feels like to be called?

He wasn't sure.

Recent tragedies had left him feeling hollow, sapping all joy out of his life. Like a man in the desert dying for lack of water, his soul thirsted for the resurrection and renewal of his wounded spirit.

"Yes, I would."

Rebecca woke with a start. Opening her eyes, she lay for a moment staring into the gloom of an unfamiliar room. As awareness returned, details from the previous hours seeped back into her sodden mind. After feeding Matthew, she'd dressed him in a fresh onesie before settling him into his bassinette. She'd sat down in a rocker near his bed, determined to keep an eye on the *boppli* through the night. But her weary bones said otherwise. She'd no more sat and begun to rock before her lids grew heavy. Within a few minutes, she'd fallen fast asleep.

"*Ach*, I can't believe I did that." Giving herself a quick slap on the cheek, she jumped up. Adjusting the illumination of a battery-powered nightlight, she peeked inside the bassinet. A set of wide blue eyes stared up at her. Fretting and wriggling, the infant gurgled and smacked his fat pink lips.

"*Gut* thing I woke up." A glance at the clock on the dresser revealed barely two hours had passed since she'd fallen asleep. Checking his diaper, she found he needed changing.

A groan slipped through her lips as she lifted him,

taking great care to properly support his wobbly little head. The long night was only beginning.

The Lord gave you what you prayed for.

Still, a stretch of time had passed since she'd last handled an infant. She'd helped when her *neffe* was born, but not as often as she would have liked. Gail and Levi had hovered close, determined to soak in every minute of parenthood. Sammy rarely had a chance to bawl before Gail swooped him up and covered his sweet face with kisses. Even young Seth took a hand in caring for his younger *bruder*. Sammy's feet barely touched the floor.

Trekking to the changing table, she made short work of the chore. Though Gail had a stack of cloth diapers, Caleb had recommended store-bought nappies for Matthew. The *boppli*'s next caregiver would most likely be *Englisch* and accustomed to disposables, so it was better to get him used to them. Balking at first, she'd come to appreciate the convenience.

By the time she'd finished, both of them were wide-awake. Heading into the kitchen, she lit a lamp before pouring a few ounces of iron-rich formula into a bottle.

"Here you go, little one."

Matthew shifted his head, refusing to latch on and nurse.

Concerned, she tried a second time. Again, the bottle was refused.

Pulse spiking, Rebecca forced herself to calm down. As a teacher, she'd had to learn to keep her cool to handle any crisis that could arise with a *youngie* at any moment. Allowing herself to get upset wouldn't do her or the *boppli* any favors.

Glancing across the living room, she noticed a thin

sliver of light beneath the guest room door. Caleb was mere steps away if she needed help. Knowing he was close calmed her jitters.

Pulling a breath, she sat down in a rocking chair near the hearth. The fire inside had burned down to embers. Glowing with heat, they lent a comfortable warmth to the brisk night air. Perhaps rocking and singing to Matthew would soothe him enough to accept his bottle.

"Hush, little baby…"

She'd barely sung a few lines when the door to the guest room opened.

Caleb stepped out. Unable to retrieve his belongings from his wrecked SUV, he'd borrowed a few items, including a pair of men's pajamas and a robe. As he was close to the same height and size as Levi, the nightclothes were a decent fit. He peered through the shadows draped throughout the living room and kitchen.

"Rebecca?" he called softly. "Is that you?"

"*Ja*, it's me." She motioned for him to join her.

Padding on bare feet, Caleb narrowed the distance between them. "I thought I heard you moving around in the nursery. I couldn't sleep, so I thought I'd join you." Taking a seat on the edge of the sofa, he leaned in. "How's Matthew?"

Happy to have the company, she adjusted the *boppli*'s blanket around his tiny body. "I changed him and tried to get him to take his bottle, but he doesn't want to eat."

Caleb's lips immediately went flat. "Is he fussing like he has a tummy ache? Does he seem lethargic or feverish?"

She shook her head. "He seemed a little uncomfortable when his diaper was wet, but once I changed it, he acted fine. He's warm but doesn't feel feverish."

"I'm no pediatrician, but I believe it's normal for a newborn to have an erratic feeding schedule for the first few days. I'd give it another hour and try again."

Rebecca barely suppressed her yawn. "I just hope I can stay awake that long. I'd forgotten how exhausting a *boppli* is."

"Surely you're not tired?" he asked, chuckling.

Somehow, she found the strength to laugh. "To the bone." Sobering, she looked at the precious bundle in her arms. "But it's worth it knowing I'm helping such an innocent little *boi*."

"That you are." He gave her a long look, admiration tingeing his words. "You're a good person, Rebecca. I wasn't thrilled I wrecked my car, but I am glad I met you and your family."

"None of us could have helped Mary or her little one the way you did. And Sheriff Miller wouldn't have let me care for him if you hadn't agreed to supervise."

His expression grew pensive. "I didn't have a reason to refuse. It's not like anyone would come looking for me if I got lost." A shrug rolled off his shoulders. "At least, not for a while anyway."

His reply prodded her curiosity. She knew Caleb had a cell phone. And he'd had access to a landline at the clinic. But she didn't remember seeing him place any calls, nor had he mentioned speaking to anyone about his unexpected delay. Though it was impossible, he seemed to have appeared out of nowhere.

"*Ach*, that can't be true," she scoffed. "Your *familie* must be worried sick. I hope you've had a chance to let them know where you are."

His expression turned pensive. "I don't have any family. My parents were killed in an accident a year ago."

* * *

Vision going misty, Caleb blinked. Emotions he believed he'd tamed bubbled to the surface. His stomach clenching, anxiety knotted his guts. He hadn't meant to revisit his past, yet somehow it had come up in conversation.

The day his life crumbled began with a phone call; his father's number popped up on his cell right in the middle of a busy shift. Pressing the phone to his ear, he'd expected to hear a familiar baritone. Instead, a female voice was on the other end. Identifying herself as a search and rescue specialist, the woman had informed him in a flat monotone that Richard and Audrey Sutter died when their small twin-engine aircraft crashed shortly after takeoff.

Numb with shock, he'd shattered into a million tiny pieces. From that point onward, almost everything was a blur. It had taken a lot of time for him to deal with his parents' complicated estate, which was still dragging its way through court.

Descending into silence, the terrible months following the double funeral unspooled across his mind's screen. After he'd laid his parents to rest, he'd found himself cast adrift in a sea of family infighting. Aunts and uncles had turned on him and each other, squabbling over the Sutter's sizable estate.

Shaking off an unexpected tremble, he brushed aside bangs damp with perspiration. His skin felt tight. Suffocating. Memories of the life he'd left behind began to overwhelm his composure.

Deep breath. Exhale.

I've got this.

No, he didn't. He was falling apart.

"Caleb, are you all right?"

Prodded for an answer, he shook his head. "I'm sorry. I didn't mean to break down like that."

"Don't be. I can listen if you need to talk."

He pulled a grimace. "I'm just wallowing in my pity." Boxing up his memories, he put them aside. "It's nothing."

Rebecca leaned back in her chair, rocking gently. Matthew snuffled in his sleep but didn't awaken. "It's *something* if it hurts you," she murmured. "And that hurts me."

Trying to relax, he settled against the sagging cushions. "Sorry. I'm not used to sharing my feelings. I've always been kind of a loner."

"Oh? You don't have siblings?"

"I'm an only child."

Sadness turned down her mouth. "I couldn't imagine not having my *schwesters* to lean on."

"My parents started their family late in life. They were in their later thirties when they got me."

"Got you?"

"I don't belong to them." Emotion grasped his throat, halting his tongue. Discovering the truth came as a shock. Stumbling across the paperwork in a safe deposit box after Richard and Audrey Sutter died had revealed the secret. "I was adopted."

Drawing Matthew closer, Rebecca cradled him like a protective mama bear. "You say that like it's a bad thing."

He rubbed his palms together to chase away the chill clutching at his insides. The cold went deep, penetrating to the core of his being. Everything he thought he knew about his life was a lie. He didn't know who he was anymore, or where he belonged. As it was, he had no one to lean on.

No one at all.

"Since I found out, I can't get it off my mind. I think about it day and night. Who were my biological parents and why didn't they want me?"

"Oh, Caleb. My heart aches for you. I can't imagine what you must be feeling."

He stared at the infant. "I guess that's why I wanted to help with the baby. This little boy deserves to know he's wanted and has a place in this world."

Chapter Five

A brief sharp shock, as though she were falling, jarred Rebecca awake. Confused and disoriented, she sat up. Rubbing the blur from her eyes, she glanced around the unfamiliar room. A dim illumination filtered through the single window. A new day was soon to begin.

"The *boppli*," she muttered, disoriented by exhaustion and lack of sleep. How could she have forgotten him? Settling her head on a downy pillow, she'd only intended to rest her eyes for a few minutes. But her tired body had other ideas. Soon, she'd fallen into a deep slumber.

A glance at the nearby clock told her at least three hours had passed since she'd last tended to the newborn. Fear laced with guilt swamped her conscience. If Matthew had cried, she hadn't heard him.

Throwing off her covers, she swung her legs over the edge of the bed. Rising from the warm mattress, she stumbled a little before catching herself. Dogged by exhaustion, she walked on numb and rubbery legs to the bassinet.

But Matthew wasn't there.

Heart missing a beat, a chill raced down her spine. "Where is he?" Pressing her palm against the mattress he'd rested on, she felt the space where his tiny body would have lain. It was cold, an indication the *boppli* hadn't been in his bed for quite a while.

A brief clatter beyond the closed door brought her head up. Other members of the household were up and moving around.

Relief filtered through her. *Thank* Gott. Knowing the infant's cries would wake her, Gail, or perhaps Amity, had most likely tiptoed in and picked up Matthew. She'd often done the same with her nephew when his parents had a hard night. Born late at night, Sammy was like an owl. Getting the little *boi* to sleep was a battle his parents fought time and time again.

Adjusting her robe, Rebecca put on a pair of slippers. Padding into the bathroom, she filled the basin with steaming water and then pressed a damp rag against her eyes. The warmth felt wonderful.

Awake and ready for a cup of coffee, she opened the door and trekked into the living room. As she suspected, Gail was at work in her kitchen. Oven stoked and lit, she was busy scooping the grounds of fragrant dark roast into an old-fashioned metal percolator. Hanging on to her long skirt, Sammy fussed to be held.

"Now Sammy, you don't need to be picked up," Gail said, glancing down. "*Mamm*'s got things to do."

Rebecca stopped midstep. Busy with her *youngie*, Gail didn't have Matthew. A quick look around told her Amity wasn't up. Nor was Florene.

Noticing her, Gail set the percolator atop the stove. "I didn't expect to see you up this early. Caleb said he hoped you'd get a few hours of sleep when he picked up Matthew."

"Caleb has Matthew?"

"*Ja.* He changed the *boppli* and made him a bottle about half an hour ago. He said you were up late, so he wanted to give you a chance to sleep."

Impressed by his willingness to help, Rebecca nodded. "How thoughtful."

Reaching for an oven mitt, Gail lifted the percolator off the stove. Setting out two large mugs, she filled both with the hot tarry liquid. "He's *gut* with little ones." A mischievous smile teased her lips. "He's a handsome fellow. If only he were Amish, he'd be a perfect *ehmann.*"

"If only he were." Rebecca rolled her eyes. "It's getting harder and harder to find a *gut* man. Which is why I have quit looking."

Gail passed her a cup. "Do you really believe that?"

Accepting the hot drink, Rebecca added cream and sugar before swallowing a mouthful. The caffeinated brew warmed her. "*Ja.* I do."

"I know Noel hurt you badly, but I don't think you should let one bad apple spoil the whole barrel. There are plenty of single men in Burr Oak. Why, if you'd let her, I'd bet Lisl Kilhefner would be able to find you a match."

Heart skipping, Rebecca's throat tightened as memories overwhelmed her. She'd envisioned spending the rest of her life with Noel once they'd wed. But after he'd discovered her health might not allow her to bear his *kinder,* he'd ended their engagement. A barren woman was a burden, not a blessing.

She stared into her half-empty cup. "The only man Lisl could find for me would be a widower who needs a *tagesmutter* for his *youngies*—or a dried-up old man who wouldn't expect *kinder* at his age. I'd like to think I was more than a convenience or a second choice."

"If you don't stop picking apart other men, you will end up old and alone."

Rebecca tightened the cloak of pity around her shoulders. "Old and alone is probably what I deserve."

Upset that she was upset, Gail stamped her foot. "That's not true! And in case you are forgetting, there are many times *Gott* granted a woman's dearest wish to bear *kinder.* Open your bible to Hebrews, to the story of Sarah. Or look to Genesis when Isaac prayed for his wife to conceive."

"I've read those passages time and time again." Squeezing her eyes shut, she pinched the bridge of her nose. "I tried to tell Noel that the Lord could still bless us," she said after her hand had dropped. "But he refused to listen. It's like his eyes and ears slammed shut. I became unworthy, of no value."

"If Noel had been any sort of man, he would have had faith the Lord would heal your womb," Gail countered. "He would have prayed for you and with you that *Gott*'s will be done. But his heart is a disbelieving one. And it is his loss. He is the one who turned away from all the wonderful things you had to offer because his faith is weak."

A sigh pressed past her lips. Still, it did nothing to lessen the pain throbbing in her heart. "I suppose that's true."

"Of course, it is. And did you ever stop and think *Gott* moved Noel out of your life because He has other plans for you?"

Rebecca shook her head. Since their breakup, she'd

felt alone, as if she'd been cast out to fend for herself. She knew it wasn't true, but uncertainty preyed on her mind. Doubt had become a sharp physical pain, stabbing hard and deep. Filling her life with other activities hadn't helped.

"I've prayed for *Gott* to give me clarity and show me that I've chosen the right path—" She shuddered from head to toe, her breath turning into a sob. "But sometimes I'm just not sure He's paying me any mind." Vaguely aware she was babbling, she let her words pour out. "I feel so alone. Like there's a dark storm brewing and it's going to swallow me up."

Closing the distance between them, Gail wrapped her in a hug. "Oh, Rebecca, that's not true," she said, speaking in a soothing tone.

Noel's rejection had stolen her sense of self-worth. Reeling, Rebecca had wrapped herself in a cloak of pity. She was praying, but the words she sent to the Lord had become hollow, meaningless.

Why should Gott *listen when I have no faith in His word?*

"Have I been so blind?" she whispered, horrified.

Tightening her grip, Gail shook her head. "You're human, as we all are. And as humans, we stumble and make mistakes. But *Gott* is always there to forgive us, to pick us up and dust us off."

"Will He forgive me?"

"Of course." Gail gave her shoulders a little squeeze. "Trust in the Lord with all your heart, and He will make straight your path." The proverb was a favorite one, quoted often.

Emotions calmed by the reassurance of touch, Rebecca released a long sigh. "*Danke.* I needed to hear that. When I do my devotional today, I will pray *Gott* gives me what He desires me to have, and not what I want for myself."

"Amen."

Unwilling to be left out, Sammy toddled up, tugging at his mother's apron.

"Hung'y," he said, giving a hopeful look. "Brekkie?" He pointed at his wide-open mouth.

Dark mood evaporating, Rebecca laughed. Sammy was learning to make himself understood. "I think he's ready to eat."

Gail bent, lifting Sammy into his high chair before adding a bib. "I know you're hungry." Fetching a fresh apple from a bowl on the counter, she peeled and sliced it into bite-sized pieces. Adding a generous dollop of homemade peanut butter to a saucer, she delivered it to her waiting child. "Eat up."

Sammy smashed his hand into the peanut butter before smearing it all over his mouth. "Mmm, *gut*!" He licked his fingers.

Gail returned to her stove. Setting a cast-iron skillet on the hottest side of the stove, she lay down thick slices of bacon. A large bowl of eggs fresh from the henhouse waited to be added to the sizzling grease. A pan of sourdough biscuits was ready to go into the belly of the beast.

The ceiling above the kitchen creaked, an indication the rest of the sleeping household was beginning to awaken. Rising over the horizon, the sun streamed through the open windows. The night was banished as the day began, bringing the promise of a fresh start.

Secure in the knowledge that she had a mighty spiritual warrior in her corner, Rebecca tucked away her insecurities. She looked forward to sitting down with her Bible and spending time in prayer.

Glancing toward the rocking chair sitting near the hearth, she didn't see the book in its usual place. It wouldn't be, as she'd loaned it to Caleb. After their conversation last night, he'd asked if he could borrow it. Sensing turmoil in his spirit, she'd gladly agreed. On the outside, Caleb appeared to be the epitome of a successful physician. But uncovering a family secret had given him a deep and troubling sense of loss.

Having gone through emotional trauma, he seemed desperate to find a sense of peace in his turbulent life. With no *familie* to fall back on, he reminded her of a drowning man—grasping on to anything solid to pull himself to safety. He needed a helping hand. Perhaps by sharing her faith and witnessing to him about the Lord, she could lead him toward salvation.

We're like two peas in a pod. Neither of us knows where we're going next.

Pulling her shoulders back, she fortified herself with a breath. "*Gott* willing, we'll both find our way."

Caleb lowered the Bible he'd borrowed from Rebecca. Unable to sleep, he'd spent the night reading. What he'd discovered within the pages was profound. For years, he'd walked through life blind to the needs of his spiritual side. Just as his mind needed the stimulation of learning and his body needed exercise, his soul needed tending.

As he held the book, an old hymn came to mind.

I once was lost...

Written long ago, the words resonated. The accident he'd cursed as bad luck had opened his eyes to a whole new life. Now that the blinders had lifted, he wanted to explore a future full of promise.

Closing the cover, he laid it aside. The jostle of his movement woke Matthew from his sleep. Wriggling, the infant gurgled.

Caleb checked to make sure he was dry. To give Rebecca a break, he'd taken over after she'd gone to bed. There was no reason for her to get up when he was awake.

"You're going to be fine," he murmured. "I promise."

The baby's plight had affected him in a way he hadn't expected. More than being responsible for the child's welfare, he felt an overwhelming sense of protection. This little soul needed his help.

A soft knock on the door lifted his gaze.

"Caleb? Are you awake?"

"Yes. Come in."

The door cracked open. Rebecca peeked inside. "Am I disturbing you?"

Rising, he scooped up Matthew. "No. We're up."

She stepped inside. "How's the *boppli*?"

Caleb patted the infant's back. "He's been a little fussy, but it's nothing to be concerned about."

"You should have woken me."

"You were sleeping so soundly it didn't seem right to wake you. I was up anyway."

Concern shadowed her face. "Something wrong?"

"Not wrong. Just a lot on my mind." Feeling he owed her an explanation for his behavior, he cleared his throat. "Just so you know, I didn't mean to spill my entire life on you last night. Once I got talking, I couldn't seem to stop." Shaking his head, he added. "That's not like me. I apologize if I got too personal."

Tipping her head, she looked at him through eyes filled with compassion. "I'm glad you felt comfortable enough to confide in me."

Relieved he hadn't offended her, he pushed out a breath. "I just wish I had known. Why did it have to be a secret?"

"Are you still angry they didn't tell you?"

He shook his head. "I was. But I don't think I am anymore."

"Oh?"

"Last night I finished Genesis and started on Exodus, the second book of the Bible."

She smiled. "That's the story of Moses."

"Yes. I guess you know he was adopted, too, a foundling raised by Egyptian royalty."

"His mother sent him down the river in a basket to save his life. She didn't want to, but she had to."

"That got me thinking. What if my mother had no choice? What if she was trying to do better for me?"

"I think it would take an incredible amount of bravery."

"Me, too." He looked at the baby in his arms, and it all made sense. "I wish I could find out who she was. I'd like to thank her."

"I will pray that you're able to do that someday."

He frowned. "I've gone as far as I can legally." Frustration tightened his tone. "The court won't unseal the records. Both sides filed an affidavit denying the release of the confidential records. The judge upheld their request." Records indicated Fort Worth was his place of birth. Past that, he had nothing else.

Giving him a knowing look, Rebecca shook her head. "*Ach*, ye of little faith. If *Gott* can move mountains, then He can give you the answers. If you look in Luke, you will see it says, 'nothing is secret, that shall not be made manifest.' I believe the Lord will give you the answers you seek in His own *gut* time."

Caleb wet his lips. Having already gone to court once, it was hard not to let negative feelings get him down. "Thank you. I hope you're right."

A new voice cut in. "You two are missing breakfast," Gail called from the kitchen.

Rebecca started. "*Ach*, that's what I'd come to tell you." Laughing, she held out her hands. "I'll take Matthew if you want to clean up."

"I do." Caleb handed the infant over before running his palms across his stubbled cheeks. He needed a shave. "I'll be right out."

"You know where we'll be."

After she'd gone, Caleb stepped into the bathroom. He washed his face, and then made short work of his whiskers with a razor he'd borrowed from Levi. Shaking the wrinkles out of yesterday's clothes, he tried to make himself presentable. A few minutes later he claimed an empty chair at the table.

"Sorry I'm late."

Rising, Gail retrieved a platter stacked with fluffy pancakes. "Help yourself, Doctor." Bacon, scrambled eggs and hash browns were also up for grabs.

"If you don't mind, I'll stick with coffee."

"Not at all."

Levi pointed at his empty plate. "I could use another helping." He forked up one of the golden orbs.

Seth grinned. "I'll have another, too."

Gail shook her head. "I don't know where you two put it. I'm convinced Wyse men have hollow legs."

Abandoning the platter, she delivered a fresh cup of coffee.

Nodding, Caleb added a splash of fresh cream to his beverage. "Thanks."

Swiping butter across the warm surface, Levi added a swirl of maple syrup. "Long day ahead." He popped a forkful into his mouth. "I'm planning to rotate the grazing land, so we'll need to get that fence repaired. Can't have those Longhorns roaming the highways."

Caleb winced. "That's entirely my fault. I have insurance if you want to file a claim."

"What you did isn't anything compared to what those Longhorns do," Seth added. "Those cows are mean. They can tear right through barbed wire."

"Really?"

Levi chuckled. "Longhorns have minds of their own. Been working with them all my life. I've never met a more stubborn critter."

"Looks like you have quite a large herd."

"Yep." Levi's mouth took on a wry twist. "And they keep us busy from sunup to sundown."

To give Rebecca and Caleb a break, Amity held Matthew. Recently changed, he'd sucked down every last drop of his formula. Doted over by a houseful of Amish women, he had the best care any baby could ever hope to receive.

"You never said where you were going, Doctor," she commented.

Caleb reached for his coffee. "Los Angeles."

"Why are you going there?" Seth asked.

"New job. I don't start for a couple more weeks, so I thought I'd get settled. I had appointments to look at rentals, but I'll need to reschedule."

Adjusting the blanket around the swaddled infant, Amity rocked the tiny bundle. "They should forgive you for being late. You were handed an unexpected delay."

Clearing the dirty dishes, Gail carried them to the sink. "I imagine you're eager to get on with your trip."

"I don't suppose it matters," he said, and finished his coffee. "No one is missing me just yet."

"Why would he want to stay?" Florene piped up. "There's nothing to do here."

"Florene, please. Don't be rude," Amity admonished.

"Just stating the truth," Florene shot back.

"As for the nothing to do," Gail said, speaking up. "You still live in this *haus* and you do have chores. The rabbits need to be fed and watered."

"And throw down some scratch for the chickens," Amity reminded.

Florene blew out a breath. "I know what needs to be done," she groused before heading out the back door. The screen slammed behind her.

"*Ach*, that girl," Amity said under her breath.

Gail watched her go. "Pray she will grow out of it."

"Speaking of chores…" Pushing away from the table, Levi stood and reached for his straw hat. "As much as I would like to sit and talk, I have work to do."

Finishing his food, Seth stood and grabbed his hat. "I'll saddle up!" Without waiting, he bounded outside.

Gail shook her head. "That *boi* loves his horses."

Levi's face took on a pensive look. "Let's just hope he doesn't want to run off to the rodeo like his old man did."

Amity passed Matthew to Rebecca. "I'd love to hold him all day, but I do need to get to town soon." Claiming her bag, she also hurried outside.

Cuddling the baby, Rebecca gave his diaper a quick check. Dry and comfortable, the little *boi* yawned. Tickling his chin, she smiled. The infant reacted with a surprised gurgle.

"*Ach*, he's a perfect angel," she cooed. "If only I could have a dozen."

Lifting her toddler out of his high chair, Gail grimaced as she inspected Sammy's messy hands and face. "And this one's a little stinker." Wearing more of his meal than he'd eaten, Sammy released a cranky wail and kicked his legs in protest.

"*Nein, mamm!*" he cried, wriggling to be set free.

Gail struggled to hold on. "Don't ask for more than you can handle," she advised. "There will be times when you'll need two sets of hands just to keep up with the one you have."

"I'll take care of him." Grinning, Levi claimed his son. "I'll give him a good dunk in one of the horse troughs."

Gail faked a frown. "The bathtub will do."

"Yes, ma'am." Holding Sammy at arm's length, Levi carried his recalcitrant child up the stairs for a bath. Sammy kicked and squealed in protest.

Caleb pushed away from the table. A feeling of discontent washed over him. He'd never been part of a busy family routine and didn't want to get in the way.

Rebecca noticed his discomfort. "Something wrong?"

"Think I'd like to stretch my legs. Is it okay if I take a walk?"

"Of course. I'd go with you if I didn't have the *boppli* to look after."

"I'll take him," Gail offered. "Levi's got Sammy, and these dishes can wait a few more minutes."

Rebecca gave her sister a grateful look. "That would be wonderful. I'd like to show Caleb the property."

Gail scooped up the baby. "I don't mind. With another on the way, I need to get used to holding a *youngie* this little again."

Rebecca stood. "*Danke*. We won't be long, I promise." Smoothing her apron into place over her ankle-length dress, she walked to the back door. "Shall we?"

Caleb followed her outside. Fenced and neatly landscaped, the backyard was an oasis of calm. A light morning breeze sifted through the trees circling the house. Overhanging limbs shaded a playground. Rope swings dangled. An old tractor tire filled with sand offered a place for children to build castles. A playhouse perched on a platform occupied the branches of a sturdy oak. The back entrance also had a shaded patio. An overhanging awning helped cut the glare of the sun.

A cobblestone walkway cut a path through the thick bluegrass. Following her through the gate, he saw the gravel drive circling through the property. Staked out near the massive barn and other sheds, animal pens were chock-full of goats, pigs, rabbits and chickens, a ready source of meat, milk and eggs. The gardens overflowed with various edibles. Feral barn cats kept the mice and other rodents at bay. Cow dogs trotted behind the hired hands, ready to go to work herding the cattle.

The entire ranch was a hive of activity. Near the employees' bunkhouse, a stout redheaded woman labored to hang the men's work clothes on a line. An older gentleman who walked with a limp and chewed on the stem of a pipe directed the hired hands through their daily activities. The whole operation appeared to be a thriving one.

Rebecca spread her hands. "What do you think?"

Head swiveling every which way, Caleb chuckled. "I'm still trying to wrap my head around the fact there are Amish in Texas. Seems like a bit of an oxymoron."

"A lot of Plain folks came from Pennsylvania seeking cheap land for farming and ranching. Back then it was a *gut* investment. My great-grandfather was among the original settlers in Burr Oak."

"Sounds like your family has quite a history here."

Rebecca nodded. "*Ja*. We do." She was about to tell him more when the unexpected crunch of tires on gravel halted the conversation.

Rounding the drive, Sheriff Miller's cruiser rolled to a stop.

Chapter Six

Pulse jumping to her mouth, Rebecca watched Sheriff Miller step out of his cruiser. Her emotions went all over the place as she wondered what news he might bring.

Straightening her shoulders, she steeled her nerve. What if he had come to take the *boppli*?

"*Guten morgen*, Evan. I wasn't expecting to see you this early."

The sheriff tipped his hat. "Morning, Rebecca. Can't say I got a lot of sleep last night. Might have even prayed a little, though I'm not sure it did any good."

She eyed his tall, sturdy frame. She'd grown up with Evan Miller and knew him to be a fine and responsible man. "The Lord's listening. Sometimes we may think we are speaking to the wind, but that's not true. *Gott* works in His time, not ours."

Miller pursed his lips. "Suppose that's true. Still, I've got to work in mine. And the delays can get frustrating when you're trying to get things moving."

"Then you've not found a place for Mary's *boppli*?"

"No. Social services just can't handle another child. If you and Dr. Sutter hadn't stepped up, there would be no place for him to go. There just aren't enough case-workers or persons willing to open their homes. On top of that, there isn't enough funding and facilities are closing. Children are being treated like criminals as they're shuffled around to hotel rooms and offices." Hands clenching, he shook his head. "I wish I had the solutions, but I just don't."

Acutely aware of his feelings, she reached out. "I know you're frustrated, but letting it overwhelm you will only make the problems seem worse. Calm down and let the Lord do His work."

"I'm trying. But I'm walking a thin line with the state as it is. It's illegal to place children with unlicensed caregivers. But because of mounting demand, children are being handed over anyway. At least I got some of the heat turned down because Mary's infant is under a physician's supervision, and you were a schoolteacher." Pausing a moment, Sheriff Miller looked to Caleb. "Can't say I'm sorry you got stuck here, Doctor."

"It's been an experience I wouldn't have wanted to miss, Sheriff," Caleb greeted affably before offering his hand. "I hope everything is okay."

Miller returned the gesture. "I was going to ask you the same thing. How is the baby?"

Caleb made a positive gesture. "Matthew's fine."

"Matthew?"

"That's what we're calling him," Rebecca explained. "No one gave him a name, so we did." Nervous, she bit her lower lip. "I hope that's all right. We had to call him something."

"I don't recall his mother saying anything about a name, so I guess it's as good as any," Miller said.

Rebecca twisted her fingers together. "Have you any

word about Mary? I've been so concerned about her. I have prayed she would find some peace."

The sheriff sketched a grimace. By the look on his face, the news wasn't positive. "Well, I can't give you any personal details except to say she's being held on a 5150 while doctors evaluate her mental state."

"What does that mean?"

"A 5150 is a psychiatric hold on persons who doctors fear are a danger to themselves or others," Caleb replied, filling in the information. "It's used when people won't willingly accept help."

"It'll only be for seventy-two hours," Miller added. "After that, doctors will decide if she's stable enough to care for herself."

"What if she isn't?"

"Then doctors will ask a judge for an emergency order of commitment at the state facility. If she's sent there, she could be gone for at least a month. Maybe longer."

"So that means we might have Matthew for quite a while?"

"I can't say for sure. It all depends on whether a case-worker can be found. And even if one shakes loose, there still has to be a safe place for the baby to go." Pausing, the sheriff added, "If you don't mind, I'm going to continue to recommend that Matthew remains in your care."

"I don't mind. I'll keep him as long as necessary."

"Glad to hear it."

Caleb cleared his throat. "Does that mean I'll be required to stay, too?"

"I don't know, Doctor. Would it be an issue?"

"If I were to be honest, no."

Miller grinned. "Good. For the time being, I'd feel better if you were here. Better safe than sorry. It'll also keep my ash from being raked into the fire if anything goes wrong."

Rebecca looked between the two men. "Would you care to see him?"

"I'd love to."

Ushering them through the back gate, she opened the screen door. Sitting at the kitchen table with a cup of coffee, Gail cradled the infant as she sang a soft lullaby.

Rebecca cocked an ear. Though her *schwester* sang in *Deitsch*, the words were familiar. Many Amish *youngies* knew the words themselves by the time they were old enough to talk.

Startled, Gail fell to silence. "Oh, my. I didn't mean for anyone else to hear my warble."

"Sounded fine to me. Sorry to walk in on you without notice."

"Not at all," Gail said. "It's *gut* to see you again, Evan."

"Haven't seen much of you since Walter Slagel's trial. I hope everything's well." After the ranch's former foreman embezzled from the business account, the sheriff had helped Gail file the complaint that would bring the thief to justice.

"*Ja.* We're getting along *gut.* I've been meaning to stop in and see how you are."

"Oh, been fine," Miller returned, keeping details to a minimum. "Just working."

As he spoke, Rebecca noticed his smile fade. *He's missing his folks.*

Born Amish, Evan had departed to pursue a career in law enforcement. His choice not to be baptized had caused a deep rift in the Miller *familie*, few of whom agreed with his desire to take a job that required him to carry a firearm. While weapons were permissible for hunting game or killing varmints, carrying a gun intended to be used against another human being was not.

Because he understood Amish ways, Plain folks trusted him to handle problems that arose in the community. He possessed the understanding an *Englischer* might not, especially when Amish youths on *rumspringa* got a little too rambunctious.

Gail also noticed. "You could come back to church, Evan."

Miller made a faint gesture of negation. "I don't think I'd be welcome."

"You belong as much as anyone," Rebecca blurted. "Just because you aren't baptized doesn't mean you won't want to be later. *Gott* understands the need for men like you to keep the peace."

"I don't want to argue it out with my *daed*, so I'll just stay away," he said, waving off the suggestion. "Besides, I don't need to sit in the pews on Sunday to talk with the Lord. He knows where I'm at and I know where He is at."

"You are always welcome to come and sit in with the group Levi leads for the hired hands on Sunday evenings," Gail suggested. "Many of them are *Englischers*, and just want to hear *Gott*'s word."

"I might do that," Miller said.

Feeling a need to change the subject, Rebecca motioned toward the stove. "Could I offer you a cup of coffee?"

"No, thank you. I don't have time. I was just doing a welfare check on the baby."

"Matthew's small, but healthy," Caleb said. "And in

case you're concerned you made a mistake, I can assure you that you did not. He's got the best possible care anyone could offer."

Miller smiled. "Amish women are excellent care-givers."

Caleb's expression grew serious. "I did not know the problems facing children in rural areas were so pressing."

"The shortages of staff, housing and funding are distressing. We could use some sort of family services center here in Burr Oak."

"I've been thinking about that, too," Rebecca said, daring to speak up. "A place where women like Mary could go to get help with their *kinder*."

Miller frowned. "It's certainly a worthy cause. But it would take a lot of time and organization. Not to mention money. And I don't know anyone who has the means to do it."

Despite his discouraging words, Rebecca's mind kept turning. It might be difficult to do, but it wasn't impossible. She intended to try.

Where there's a will, there's a way.

The sheriff had barely finished speaking when the two-way microphone clipped on his shoulder crackled. A blast of static followed by garbled words filled the air.

Everyone froze.

Rebecca gave him a nervous look. "Is something wrong?" The few words she'd made out didn't sound promising.

"Excuse me. I need to take this." Stepping aside, Miller cocked his head to listen to the message sent out by the dispatcher. As the unintelligible words poured out, his face paled. Squeezing the mike, he sent a quick reply. "Ten-four. Understood. Yes, I'm here with Dr. Sutter now. I'll bring him as soon as I can." His tone held a note of alarm.

Rebecca's heart smashed into her rib cage. Breath drizzling away, fear circled her spine with chilly fingers. A sense of helplessness washed over her.

Gott, let everything be all right.

"Evan, what's happening?"

The sheriff turned to face them. A grim cast darkened his expression.

"Dr. Gordon collapsed a few minutes ago. They think he's having a heart attack."

Eyes closed, Dr. Gordon lay back in bed. Head propped up on fluffy pillows, his complexion was pale and drawn. "Well," he demanded in a croaky voice. "What's the diagnosis?"

Caleb lifted his stethoscope away from the old man's chest. "Chest pain or discomfort?"

Gordon shook his head. "No." As he sucked in air, his voice was close to soundless.

"Feeling weak, light-headed or faint?"

"A little weak."

"Pain or discomfort in the jaw, neck or back?"

"I hurt all over," the older man groused. "I've had arthritis for the last forty years."

"Pain or discomfort in one or both arms or shoulders?"

Dr. Gordon frowned. "There's nothing on me that doesn't hurt at my age."

"Shortness of breath?"

"Only from answering your ridiculous questions," Dr. Gordon retorted behind flaring nostrils.

Caleb refrained from rolling his eyes. The worst patients in the world were other doctors. Treating them was harder than raising the dead.

"Well, aside from being the most mulish patient I've ever seen, I think it is safe to say you didn't have a heart attack."

"Then what was it?"

"Mostly likely you collapsed from exhaustion brought on by overwork and a lack of sleep." Eyeing the old man's thin figure, he added, "How long has it been since you've had a day off?"

Dr. Gordon frowned with offense. "I never take a day off," he said, speaking as if the notion were an insult. "I have patients to see."

"Seven days a week?"

"People don't stop getting sick because it's a weekend."

"You do have a nurse practitioner. Karyn can see patients."

"Yes, I am aware," Dr. Gordon shot back. "And you know she can't diagnose or prescribe medicines in this state. As much as I trust her judgment, the state requires her to work under a physician's supervision."

Caleb sighed. Yes, he did know.

"Well, you're not going to be available for a while. You need to get away from the clinic at least a week. Two would be even better."

The old man frowned. "Impossible." Sitting up, he threw aside his blanket. Climbing to his feet, he managed a few steps before he began to wobble.

Caleb offered a steadying hand. "You're in no shape to argue, much less go back to work." Guiding his patient back into bed, he tugged the covers back over the old man's frail body. "As your doctor, I'm ordering you to stay in bed and rest." Narrowing his eyes, he added, "Don't make me contact the medical board."

Eyes widening, Dr. Gordon stiffened. "You would threaten my license?" Despite his recalcitrant manner, worry grated in his tone.

Knowing he'd touched a nerve, Caleb backed off. He hated playing the bad guy, but he also had to do what was necessary to protect his patient. "I don't want to, but I have to do what is best for your health."

"But—but what about my patients?" A visible tremble moved him. "Someone has to see them. They have nowhere else to go."

"Is there no other doctor nearby who can help while you're in recovery?"

"No." Disappointment washed over Dr. Gordon's wrinkled face. "I've been trying for years to recruit young doctors. So far, few have responded. I thought I had one…" His voice trailed off.

"Oh? Who?"

"A young fellow in Arizona, Dr. Oliver Wiley. He was supposed to show up on the fifth, but never arrived." Expression turning inward, the old man's disappointment visibly deepened. "I guess he changed his mind." Losing strength, he dropped back against his pillows. His face, heavily lined, looked haggard and hopeless.

The ache behind Dr. Gordon's words was hard to miss. The older man was tired and wanted to slow down, but loyalty to his community and patients kept him working long past the time when he should have been enjoying his golden years. Such selflessness had driven him to the edge of a total collapse.

Seeking a solution, Caleb did a few mental calculations. His SUV would be out of commission for at least two weeks, maybe more. Since he already knew he'd miss the appointments he'd made to tour a few apartments in Los Angeles, he could cancel. He could always reschedule once he had a firmer grip on his timeline.

I could hang around and help.

The idea proved attractive. Knowing Sheriff Miller had a lot on the line, it would still allow him to watch over Matthew. While Caleb didn't think the infant's heart murmur was a problem, he did get the feeling his elderly colleague wouldn't be inclined to follow orders unless someone kept a strict eye on him.

"Listen, I have a little time on my hands. If you like, I could stick around and see your patients."

Dr. Gordon brightened. "You would do that for an old man?"

Warmed by his colleague's enthusiasm, Caleb leveled his gaze. At this point, walking away wasn't an option. If nothing else, his profession preached not only healing but compassion. While some people might have rightly accused him of being unfriendly and standoffish, he wasn't a coldhearted jerk. California could wait.

"Yeah. I will." Holding out a hand, he added, "Now keep in mind it's nothing permanent. I do have commitments elsewhere. But you could consider it a favor for a colleague."

That, and the fact it would give him a little more time to spend with Rebecca and the young charge who'd stolen everyone's hearts.

The elderly man presented a grin. "Can you start tomorrow?"

"Calm down. I'm sure we'll hear something soon." Stomach twisted into knots, Rebecca forced herself to take a deep breath. "I wish I could. I saw Dr. Gordon yesterday. He looked so frail. What if Caleb hadn't been there to help with Mary's delivery?"

"I know you are worried. But fretting won't add a single hour to your life."

Anxious and unsettled, she clasped her hands to calm an inner tremble. "I can't help it. When bad things happen, I feel so helpless."

Unable to sit another second, she rose. Crossing the living room, she tugged back the curtain. Peering across the front yard, she searched the driveway. It had stayed empty since Sheriff Miller whisked Caleb away after receiving the emergency notice. The hands of the clock had shifted as morning turned into afternoon. Hours had gone by, yet they'd not heard a single word.

"We all do." Behind her, Gail's voice was firm. "Therefore, keeping our eyes on *Gott* is so important. We are to cast our anxieties to Him when life is in turmoil."

"I know these things and I know what I should be doing. But my mind seems so unsettled lately. It's like the ground shifts constantly. I can't keep my footing. Each step seems more treacherous than the last." Sighing, she let the curtain drop. Her out-of-control emotions left her feeling dizzy and ashamed. She'd prayed for peace, but her mind wouldn't rest.

"Sit down. I'm sure we'll have word soon."

Rebecca complied. "It's times like this I'd like to have my own cell phone." Reaching out, she rocked the cradle holding little Matthew. Soothed by the motion, the *boppli* slept peacefully. Having learned of his mother's status during Sheriff Miller's visit, Rebecca wondered what future Mary might choose for her *sohn*.

Would she try to keep him? Or would she choose to give him up for adoption?

He's barely a day old. Yet already his future is in turmoil. What will his tomorrow bring?

The answer was not clear. It might not be for a long time.

The commotion of barking dogs followed the sound of a vehicle's engine. The melee filtered through the open windows, shattering the peace of the afternoon.

Rebecca cocked her head. The canines rarely set up such a racket unless strangers came onto the property. A car door slammed. A loose board on the front deck creaked under a heavy step. A knock at the front door followed.

"I'll get it."

Smoothing wrinkles out of her apron, she checked her *kapp* to ensure it was pinned on straight. A familiar face greeted her with a smile.

"Caleb, you're back." Stepping aside to allow him entry, she pressed a hand against her middle. A warm sensation fluttered through her stomach. Glancing through the open door, she saw the van he'd intended to rent the day before.

"You got your vehicle."

"Yes. Sheriff Miller arranged it while I was at the clinic. Can't say I'd imagined driving a cargo van, but it is nice to have wheels again. I even managed to pick up my things from the mechanic's shop."

"How're the repairs on your SUV going?"

"Parts are ordered, but it will be off the road awhile."

"We've been waiting for word about Dr. Gordon all afternoon," Gail prodded. "How is he?"

"I'm happy to say he's going to be fine."

"Thank *Gott*. We all prayed he would be all right."

"Was it a heart attack?" Rebecca asked.

"No. His collapse was brought on by exhaustion. Simply put, he's just worked himself to the bone."

Relief allowed her to relax. "*Ach*, that poor man. Even the Lord advocates for rest, but Dr. Gordon doesn't seem to know how."

"I understand he doesn't want to let his patients down. It's admirable. But it's not realistic."

"At his age, he should be retired and enjoying his golden years," Gail commented.

Caleb shook his head. "He's a stubborn old fellow. He isn't going to rest just because I say so."

"Knowing Dr. Gordon, that sounds about right."

"The thing is, I'm concerned he will have a heart attack for real if he doesn't slow down."

"Is there anything you can do?"

"Kind of." Chuckling, he went on to add, "We made a deal."

Surprise crinkled her brow. "Did you?"

"Yes. I'm going to cover for him at the clinic while he rests." He jerked his thumb toward his rental. "I've rented a room in town, so it's all set."

Rebecca's breath caught in her throat. "You're not staying here?"

He offered a wry half smile. "I thought would be presumptuous to invite myself to stay longer than I already have."

"But what about Matthew?" she queried, disappointed.

"The clinic closes around five. I can drive over and check him in the evening."

She nodded. His pending departure left her feeling

forlorn and wretched. "I suppose it would be more convenient if you were in town."

"There's no reason for you to spend money on a hotel room when we have a guest room, Doctor," Gail said, stepping neatly into the conversation. "And you can reach town fairly quickly in a gas-powered vehicle, so why not just stay here?"

"You wouldn't mind?"

Gail didn't blink. "Not at all."

"And you are supposed to be supervising Matthew's care." Eager for him to accept, Rebecca added, "If nothing else, it would keep Sheriff Miller out of trouble."

"Well, I wouldn't want to cause the sheriff any more trouble than he's already got."

"Then it's settled. You'll stay."

Relenting, he held up a hand. "I'll accept. But only on one condition."

Barely able to breathe, Rebecca nodded "And that is?"

"I'd like to get a Bible." As he paused to clear his throat, his manner turned shy, more respectful. "Maybe you could recommend which one a new Christian should buy."

Chapter Seven

The gentle slopes of the Texas plains stretched as far as the eye could see. Miles of buffalo grass and other flora mingled with stubby mesquite bushes. Tires skimming over a gentle rise in the road, Caleb glimpsed water towers and other buildings on the rolling horizon.

"I didn't realize how remote some of these little towns are."

Sitting beside him with her hands folded in her lap, Rebecca cocked her head. "Just think what it must have been like when our ancestors crossed these plains. I can't even imagine the hardships those people must have faced traveling by wagon to settle new land."

"Seems like people were made of sterner stuff back then." Buzzing down the driver's side window, Caleb tipped back his head. Skin warmed by the sun, a light breeze tousled his hair. Pilot-style sunglasses shielded his eyes from the glare emanating from the black asphalt. Having learned his lesson about twisty Texas highways, he was careful to adhere to the speed limit.

"I recall you mentioning your family was some of the first Amish to settle here."

"*Ja*, they were. They set down their first soddy right where the house stands now."

"I'm sorry—what?"

"A soddy is blocks of sod lifted from the earth. Prairie grass is thickly rooted and can be dug quickly for construction. Once folks had a basic shelter in place, they could gather better materials to build sturdier homesteads." Lifting a hand, she pointed in the distance. "See those trees?"

Caleb glanced at the landscape before returning his gaze to the road. Thick copses of trees occupied the wide-open space, growing along old streams and riverbeds. Perched on a solid trunk, their heavy branches spread a crown of dark green foliage.

"Yes. I see them. Are those what's planted around the ranch?"

"Those are Burr Oaks. They helped contribute to the survival of the settlers by providing the materials they needed to build their cabins. And when they are planted around a property, they offer shade from the heat. They also give us a break from the spring winds."

"I guess it was a matter of adapting to survive back then."

"Isn't that the way it's always been?"

Caleb tightened his grip on the steering wheel. "I suppose. Life throws out its challenges and we have to duck and weave to avoid the pitfalls."

"Or we can pray. And you don't even have to ask *Gott* for strength or courage. All you have to do is lay your troubles in His hands and let Him take care of the problem."

"You make it sound so easy to be a Christian."

Lowering her gaze, Rebecca went silent.

"Did I say something wrong?"

She shook her head. "*Nay*. But I must address what you said, and with complete candor."

"Okay…"

"Living by *Gott*'s word isn't easy. It's hard."

"Because you're Amish?"

"*Nein*. Because we're human. And even though we might believe ourselves strong in faith, it's easy to fall prey to temptation. Sin exists. And every time we sin, we take ourselves further away from the Lord's reach. People might not understand, but that's why Plain folks who are baptized eschew a lot of modern conveniences."

Caleb mulled her words. As an *Englischer*, he'd grown up with luxuries at hand. "I was curious about that."

Rebecca cocked her head. "Think about it. Electricity powers things like televisions."

"I guess so."

"You may think watching a television show is harmless. But what message is it sending to our *youngies*?"

Caleb kept his eyes on the road. "I never really thought about it. I admit, there's a lot of garbage in this world. Garbage I don't think I'd want my kid to see."

"Oh, make no mistake. They will see it, and they will mimic it."

He glanced her way. "That *rumspringa* thing, right? Like Florene is doing with her clothes and cell phone? How does she even charge that thing?"

She laughed. "It's pretty simple. We don't have electricity in the *haus*, so she uses a portable generator. They can be charged with solar panels, so a lot of Amish do use them. They're also handy for our *Englisch* workers if they need to power batteries for tools they use."

"I guess that makes sense, in a round about way. But if the Amish really want to keep their young people away from things like that, why give them the chance to run wild?"

"We don't baptize our *youngies*, so they are not yet members of the church. Therefore, they are given free will to explore the *Englisch* world so that they might make an informed decision as to whether they want to remain in the community. If they choose to be baptized, it is a commitment expected to last a lifetime."

"Did you find it hard to go back after your *rumspringa*?"

Her answer was almost immediate. "*Nein*. I knew I would be staying in the church. Noel and I chose to get baptized when we got engaged as our promise to each other."

Caleb's brows rose. He'd had no idea Rebecca was spoken for. Upon meeting her, he'd assumed her to be single. "I don't believe I've met him."

Expression shutting down, a little chuff slipped through her lips. "We are no longer together. We ended our engagement quite a few years ago."

"I'm sorry to hear that."

"It was the right decision." She released a long breath. "We were not suited for each other. Better to know it beforehand than after the wedding. After that, we'd have been stuck with each other."

"I take it the Amish do not allow divorce."

"When we take our help-meet, it is for life."

"What if you're not compatible?"

"One can choose to abandon a spouse, but few rarely do because they don't want to be shunned. But even if one does leave, the abandoned party is not allowed to remarry."

"Seems a little harsh."

"To an *Englischer*, it may be. But for us, it's a reason to work harder together to sort out our differences. Make no mistake about it. Amish couples have their share of squabbles. But the Lord warns us not to let the sun go down on our anger. If we are strong in the word, the day will end with kind words and kisses."

Caleb grinned. "Kisses are a nice way to end the day."

Rebecca covered her face with her hands as a blush reddened her cheeks. "Oh, my. I am so sorry. I didn't mean to speak in such an intimate way."

Suddenly aware of how close she sat, he kept his grip on the steering wheel. He hadn't failed to notice how his heart rate bumped up a notch when she was near. And why shouldn't it? Rebecca was an attractive woman. Long hair tucked neatly under her *kapp*, a few stray tendrils curled around her delicate ears. She looked wholesome and adorable.

And she was entirely out of his reach.

Slipping behind the detached mask of a professional, he said, "I went to med school. I know all about the birds and the bees."

She lowered her hands, peering over the tips of her fingers. "Well, I usually don't speak about those things with strange men."

"I'd hope by now we could call ourselves friends."

Giving him a long look, she nodded. *"Ja,"* she said, and her nose wrinkled most enticingly. "We are."

The conversation fell to a lull as they rolled into town.

"I think the bookstore is just up here," he said and

pointed. If he recalled correctly, it was called Praise the Word.

"It is. I'm surprised you noticed."

He laughed. "Hard to miss things when you're trotting through town in a wagon. I saw a couple of other places I'd like to visit, too."

"Most people get annoyed traveling at a snail's pace."

"I rather liked it because it gave me a chance to look around and note interesting landmarks."

Guiding his rental into a parking space, he shifted into Park and killed the engine. He couldn't wait to pick his Bible and begin his studies. The previous night had revealed a lot was missing from his life. He prayed God would help him find the answers he sought.

"How do I know which one to choose?" As he browsed through the selections, Caleb's expression turned into a question mark. "There's so many I don't even know where to begin. Which one do you use?"

Quickly scanning the shelves, Rebecca pointed. "Most Amish use the King James Bible. I like the study version."

Caleb reached for the book. "Then that's the one I want."

"It is a *gut* choice for a new believer, as it also offers archaeological insights."

"Really?"

"*Ja.* I love being able to understand the historical context of the texts and more about the times in which they were written. Once you delve into the past, you realize how reliable *Gott*'s word is. Civilizations have risen and fallen, but His words have not changed for thousands of years." Drawing in a breath, she gazed around. "There's nothing I love more than getting new books. It's like receiving a gift every time I open one."

"I'm curious to know what kind of books the Amish read."

She laughed. "I guess *Englischers* imagine that all we get to read are our Bibles or the *Budget* newspaper. The truth is I love Jane Austen and devoured all her books when I was younger."

He grinned. "So, are you a Darcy fangirl?"

Rebecca faked a sniff of disdain. "Darcy is a snob, but the character does grow on you because of his ability to recognize his foibles. I like that Elizabeth stands up to him and makes him think about how he treats others."

"In other words, it takes a good woman to turn a man around." Pausing, he added, "Kind of like you did me."

Her brows rose. "*Ach*, Caleb. I did no such thing. You're a doctor, a man with a *Gott gegeben* gift to heal the sick. I saw how you helped Mary. Now you're helping Dr. Gordon. And just by watching you with Matthew, I can tell you're a man with a *kind* heart. I've not seen you hesitate once to help since you've been here."

Gazing at the book, he blew out a breath. "To tell you the truth, there are times when I was a self-centered jerk. This last year—" He shook his head. "All I did was feel sorry for me."

Sensing his disquiet, Rebecca lay a hand on his arm. The conflict he felt inside was readily apparent. "You weren't who you thought you were."

"I was angry Richard and Audrey didn't tell me." Throat momentarily tightening, he blinked hard and shook his head. "I'll never know the details, but I do know it's time to let the dead rest in peace. They deserve my forgiveness. Otherwise, how can I ask God to forgive my trespasses?"

The grief behind his words touched her deeply. "Just as we forgive others, we must also forgive ourselves."

Conflict fading, Caleb's gaze rose to meet hers. "I can't tell you how long I've been looking for these answers."

Caught in the emotion of the moment, Rebecca gazed back. A gentle pulse of understanding passed between them. His internal barriers were down. The meeting of their eyes wholly exposed him to her. More intimate than a kiss, it was the first tentative touch of one soul reaching out to another.

The sound of heavy footsteps came to an abrupt halt behind them.

"May I help you find something?"

The fragile connection between them shattered.

Embarrassed to be caught standing so close to a man who was not her *ehmann*, Rebecca stepped back. The owner of the store, Elias Branch, was elderly, Amish, and a stickler for propriety.

"No—no, Mr. Branch. I think we've found the one we want."

Elias Branch gave a suspicious look. Disapproval was written in the deep lines around his puckered mouth. "Samuel wouldn't approve of you walking about with an *Englischer*, Rebecca."

A curious inward tremble moved her. *Surely, he doesn't think we're together?*

Returning a frown, she hurried to quash the notion. "I assure you Dr. Sutter isn't my beau, Mr. Branch. He's my *freund* and I was helping him pick out a Bible." She hoped nipping the notion in the bud would stop the rumor before it got out of control. Her reputation had already suffered enough damage in the wake of her breakup with Noel. If folks believed she was stepping out with an *Englischer*, she'd lose all respectability. She and Caleb could be friends, but nothing more. The slightest hint of romance between them was strictly *verboten*.

Passing a final glance between them, the old man shook his head. The expression on his face said he didn't believe her. Still, he chose not to pursue the matter.

"Well, he'll need to be paying for it before he goes to reading it."

"I certainly do intend to pay," Caleb said, attempting to smooth things over. "Do you accept credit cards?"

"Cash only." Limping toward the counter, the old man rang up a total on his register. The old push-button machine had to be at least ninety years old. The *Ordnung* might have allowed modern equipment to be used for business purposes, but many of the older Amish business owners eschewed anything requiring electricity.

"I can do that." Digging out his wallet, Caleb handed over a hundred-dollar bill.

Elias Branch counted out his change. "I hope you intend to live by the Lord's word," he said before slipping the purchase into a paper bag.

"I assure you my intention is sincere, sir."

Keeping a respectful distance from each other, they departed.

"Haven't felt like that since I was sixteen and on my first date," Caleb commented as they stepped outside.

"Don't be too hard on Elias. In his day a proper Amish *fraulein* wouldn't be caught alone in the company of an *Englischer*."

He gave her a troubled look. "I hope I'm not breaking some rule by taking you out in public."

"It's perfectly all right for us to be out together. It's not like we're out on a date or anything like that."

Tension easing, Caleb jerked his thumb toward a coffee shop down the street. "Would it be okay if I asked you to have a cup of coffee? I haven't had anything since this morning. I'm about to drop from lack of caffeine."

Rebecca hesitated. "I'd like to, but I promised Gail we wouldn't be gone long."

"I trust your sister knows how to handle a baby. Besides, we never had time to grab lunch yesterday."

She laughed. "We did get sidetracked."

"We can grab a cup and go if it makes you feel better."

"I guess it would be okay to take another half hour. Gail said not to hurry. And she has Ruth Weaver to help. Matthew is in *gut* hands."

"Then it's settled." Caleb tucked his purchase under his arm. "Shall we?"

The main street was a treat for buyers seeking Amish crafts. Sidewalks were a showplace, displaying a variety of handmade furniture by master woodworkers. Women talented in needlework sold beautiful quilts and other fabulous decorative items. There was even an apothecary's shop offering natural remedies. Visitors handing over their dollars to the locals were easy to spot. Most had out-of-state license plates.

Walking side by side, they paused at a window to browse items offered for sale.

Caleb pointed to a selection of quilts and other linens embroidered with fine stitching. "The work is exquisite. It must take months to create these."

"Aye, they do."

Leaving the display, they continued their walk toward the coffee shop.

"I never knew such a jewel existed," he said, changing the subject. "Didn't ever think there was much to these little towns. Burr Oak is kind of like a mirage, rising out of the desert. It's fascinating to find a different culture living here."

"Admittedly, we're not as large of a settlement as you would find in Pennsylvania or Ohio. But as people migrated, they splintered off from the original groups to form new branches."

His brow crinkled. "All Amish aren't the same?"

"In some ways, *ja.* In others, *nein.*"

"Now I'm getting confused."

"The Amish live by the *Ordnung.* That's a set of rules we must all agree to live by if we wish to be a part of the community. But there are differences. Some are stricter than others."

His gaze sharpened. "How so?"

"Some allow the use of certain technologies in their businesses and others do not. Some groups have a dedicated building for church—like we do here. And others adhere to the tradition of neighbors hosting services on a rotating basis. We also have Sunday school for our *youngies,* whereas others do not."

"Can they choose how they want to live?"

"Not exactly. It depends on the bishop and the church elders. They meet regularly to assess whether something would be a benefit to the community. If it does, the *Ordnung* is amended. If it's not, then an explanation is given as to why it was rejected."

"Say some folks don't agree. What next?"

"If an agreement isn't reached, a group may decide to relocate and establish their own congregation. A new bishop will be appointed, and they will create the *Ordnung* they wish to live by."

"So even though you share common origins, traditions can vary by geography?"

"*Ja*. But at the core, we're not so different. The glue that binds us together is our love for *Gott*. We desire to live in a way that pleases and serves our Lord."

The conflict drained from his face. "I like the way you explain things. Simple and straightforward."

"I used to be the schoolmistress. Teaching was my job."

"Was?"

Rebecca nervously laced her fingers together. The conversation had circled to a touchy subject.

Is it any of his business?

Probably not.

But there was no reason to lie. She had nothing to be ashamed of.

"Noel didn't want a working *ehefrau*, so I resigned from my position as our wedding date approached. He wanted me to stay home and raise our *youngies*."

Surprise etched his expression. He blinked as if dismayed. "And you were okay with him telling you to give up your job and stay home?"

"Why wouldn't I be? The Bible teaches us to submit to our *ehmann* the way we submit to *Gott*. And he was right to ask. We planned a large *familie*."

Caleb tightened his grip on his new purchase. "I guess if you live by what's in the Bible that makes sense."

"Our *youngies* are the foundation of our way of life. It binds us together and makes our community stronger. The Lord teaches us that through His Word."

His tense expression lessened. "I have so much to learn."

She offered a smile. "If it makes you feel better, a *frau* oversees her household. And a woman's place is beside a man, not behind him. And women are not less important for staying home and raising their *youngies*. Women work just as hard as men—sometimes harder."

"I won't argue with you there."

Recalling the loss of what might have been, she sighed. "I was looking forward to sharing my life with him, but it wasn't to be." Regret circled her heart, squeezing hard with cruel talons. "I'll never have another chance to marry now."

"Don't say that. You'll meet someone else. Soon, I'm sure."

Rebecca shook her head. *"Nein."* Aching with the loss of what could have been, she added, "Noel broke up with me because I can't have *kinder.*"

Chapter Eight

"Please forget what I said. I have no idea why I told you that…"

Barely able to make eye contact, Rebecca took a quick sip of her mocha cappuccino. Mortified she'd shared such a personal detail, she left untouched the banana-nut muffin she'd selected. Full of painful knots, her stomach couldn't handle a single bite of the delicious treat.

Perched on a stool across from her, Caleb picked at the edges of an apple fritter.

"An infertility issue is nothing to be ashamed of. I'm going to assume it is something you have spoken to a physician about."

Hesitant to continue, Rebecca glanced around the quaint little coffeehouse. Decorated in a simple manner it was a popular stop on Main Street for locals and tourists alike. Customers gathered around other tables, engrossed in conversation.

No one gave them a second glance.

Forcing herself to relax, she nodded. "*Ja*. I've seen Dr. Gordon. He diagnosed my endometriosis."

"And he told you that you'd never have children?"

"Based on his examinations, he said it was advanced and I would have issues with—" Unable to say the words, her face warmed with embarrassment.

"Conception," Caleb finished.

Lowering her gaze, Rebecca nodded. *"Ja."*

"It's nothing to be embarrassed about. A lot of women suffer from the issue. And I am a medical professional, so it's nothing I haven't heard about."

Lifting her cup, Rebecca sipped the hot brew. Normally she enjoyed the treat. But the liquid didn't mix well with the bitter acid churning in her stomach.

"It's not a thing I want to be shared," she said, speaking in a low tone. "In the Amish community, a woman's ability to have *kinder* is part of her value to her future *ehmann*. As it is, I have no expectation any man would want me."

Caleb's brow took on a row of deep furrows. "Is that an Amish roundabout way of saying you're worthless?"

"Ja. It's only natural for a man to choose an *ehefrau* who can give him *sohns* to carry on the *familie* name."

"And that's why your fiancé broke off the engagement?"

Remorse choked her. "It is. I'm ashamed to say it, but I begged him to let the doctors help us with the issue. But he said *nein*, that *Gott* had judged me unfit to bear *kinder*."

"That's just cruel on every level."

"Noel's *familie* comes from the Old Order. Many of the older generations have the mindset that seeking help for fertility issues is unacceptable, the Devil's work of offering false hope."

"I don't understand. The Amish do see doctors, right?"

"Ja, we do. But many Plain folks prefer to seek natu-

ral treatments for ailments before turning to a medical professional. And some believe *Gott* is the only cure and won't go for treatment at all."

Shaking his head, Caleb pursed his lips. "Excuse me for saying so, but that sounds a bit backward."

"You can't blame them. The Bible does say prayer will save one who is sick."

"Yet your fiancé didn't believe you could pray the affliction away," he countered softly. "What does that say for his faith?"

"I don't know. I admit, my faith has wavered…" Catching what had come out of her mouth, she winced. "I probably shouldn't have said that."

"Why?"

Rebecca glanced toward the Bible he'd purchased. Still wrapped in its brown paper bag, it sat near his elbow. "Because it makes me a hypocrite. Witnessing to you about the glory of *Gott* even as I've questioned Him myself. What kind of Christian am I if I'm not confident and strong in the faith I want to share with others? The Lord says one who doubts is like a wave of the sea that is driven by the wind. That person must not suppose that he will receive anything."

Pushing aside his barely eaten dessert, Caleb propped his elbows on the table. "Well, it probably isn't my place to say it, but I will. I think you are the luckiest woman alive."

"You do?"

He nodded. "Not only does this Noel guy sound like a jerk, but I'd also say he was the one who wasn't strong in his faith. I haven't read every page of the Bible, but I do think that a good man—a godly man—would support the woman he loved. If that meant prayer, or even holding your hand while you saw a physician who could help you, then a true man would be right beside you every step of the way."

Amazement dropped her jaw. "Gail told me the same thing."

Caleb raised his gaze, refusing to blink. "Your sister is a wise woman. If I were you, I'd take her word." Giving her a warm look, he added, "You deserve a man who adores you and accepts you just the way you are."

"If he exists, I'd like to meet him."

The corners of Caleb's mouth rose. "I think you will. Soon."

Moved by the sincerity in his words, Rebecca felt a curious sensation circle her spine. A warmth like the sun breaking through stormy clouds spread through her.

"Your words might cheer me if my prospects weren't so narrow. As it is, no one's asked me on a walkabout in years."

"I asked you out and you said yes."

"I don't think coffee with a *freund* counts as a date," she said, emphasizing the masculine usage of the word.

A smile continued to tease his lips. "It's a start."

Breaking their eye lock, Rebecca lifted her cup. Her breath was caught in half a hitch, making it almost impossible to breathe. There was no denying Caleb was a handsome fellow. His search for faith, the willingness to believe in *Gott*, made him all the more attractive.

Temptation hovered like the forbidden apple.

But if she wavered, she knew she would fall.

She steeled her resolve. "If I were younger and more naive, I might be flattered by your flirting."

"The Amish don't allow flirting?" Reclaiming his pastry, he pinched a bite to nibble.

"I meant dating an *Englischer*. It's not allowed."

"At all?"

"Nein."

"Can't you bend the rules? Just a little?"

"Nein. We wouldn't be able to see each other unless you were Amish—or had close relatives who were. Even then you'd have to declare your intention to be baptized."

"Could I do that?" he asked. "Be baptized in your faith?"

His question caught her off guard. "I—I'm not sure. All I can say is it doesn't happen often. Certainly, it would be something you'd have to speak with the bishop about."

"I see." His gaze captured hers again, probing deep. "Would you ever consider leaving the church?"

"Never. When I was baptized, I meant it to be for the rest of my life."

"Not even for love?"

"I couldn't. Ever." The words stuck in her throat, forcing her to push them out. "It would be misleading to say anything else."

Disappointment laced its way through his expression. "At least you're honest. I appreciate that." Dropping his gaze, he checked his watch. "Looks like we've used that half hour." Claiming his cup, he gulped down the last of his coffee. "Shall we go? I'd like to check on Dr. Gordon to make sure he's following orders."

Sensing his retreat, Rebecca rose from her chair. She hated cutting him off like that. But the invisible line she'd drawn was necessary. Encouraging him would be disastrous on so many levels. Intuition warned her to step back, and let temptation find another path to walk.

It's for the best.

"Could we stop at the market, too? I should pick up a few things for Matthew."

A nod indicated his agreement. "Of course." Tucking his parcel under his arm, Caleb led the way to the exit. Pushing it open, he stepped aside. "Please," he said, allowing her to go first.

Without glancing ahead, Rebecca hurried onto the sidewalk. A sudden collision bought her to a dead halt.

"Oh, my heavens!" a man exclaimed.

Stumbling back, Rebecca focused on the figure she'd crashed into. Heavy, with silver hair and a reddish complexion, his features were clear and well-defined. His upper lip was neatly shaved, and his beard was full and thick. A hawklike gaze peered from behind thick black frames.

"I am so sorry, Bishop," she stammered, addressing the familiar figure. "Please, pardon me for being so inattentive."

Bending to retrieve the items he'd dropped, Clark Harrison shook his head. "It's quite all right. I was just on my way in for a cup of coffee before heading to a church meeting."

"Caleb and I stopped in for a cup ourselves," she said, uncertain why she felt the need to explain being away from her charge. "We were just leaving."

Bishop Harrison's eyes widened. "Would that be Dr. Sutter?"

"Ja. But how—"

"I spoke to Sheriff Miller not an hour ago. He told me about the *boppli* you've taken in. He was relieved the *youngie* had a place to go."

The unexpected praise warmed her. *"We're willing*

to help in any way needed." Turning, she acknowledged Caleb's presence. Standing quietly, he waited to be introduced. "But I wouldn't have been able to take Matthew without Dr. Sutter's help."

"Ah, so here's the man himself. I've been wanting to meet you, Doctor." The older man offered his hand. "It was *gut* of you to volunteer to help such an innocent little soul."

Caleb accepted his gesture. "Happy to."

"And Evan says you will be working at the clinic, too. Terrible news about Dr. Gordon. Was it a heart attack?"

"No. Just exhaustion."

"I'm sure David needs the rest. He may be *Englisch*, but he's lived a more pious life than some whose names I'll not mention. I pray the Lord will send a godly man to ease his burden."

Looking between the two men, Rebecca laced her fingers together. "He often mentions he'd like to retire and spend more time with his *enkelkinder*."

Caleb's grip tightened on the Bible tucked beneath his arm. "I'll add him to my prayers." He gazed around the shaded sidewalk. "Whoever accepts his offer will find your community delightful. It looks like a lovely place to settle down and raise a family."

"Speaking of *familie*, Sutter is an Amish name." Narrowing his eyes, Clark Harrison peered over the edge of his glasses. "Are any of them in these parts your kin?"

"I don't believe so."

"Are you sure? For some reason, you look familiar. I can't say where, but I know I've seen your face before."

Caleb raised his brows. "I assure you no one wears this face but me. And I've never spent time in Burr Oak before today."

Bishop Harrison blinked, incredulous that he was mistaken. "Well, never mind. At my age, faces begin to blend." Waving a hand toward his forehead, he made a tsking sound. "And do excuse me for cutting you short. I need to grab my coffee and get going." Bidding them a good day, he hurried into the coffee shop.

Rebecca watched him go. "I do believe you fuzzled the bishop."

"I didn't mean to." Gaze going inward, Caleb's expression turned contemplative.

"Is something wrong?"

"The bishop said he'd seen my face before. I wonder if it's possible."

Curiosity prodded. "If what's possible?"

He sucked in a breath, then let it out. "That somewhere out there, someone looks like me."

Hands tucked behind his neck, Caleb lay on a blanket in the backyard. Spread on a cushion of thick bluegrass, it offered a comfortable place to stretch out and rest. Eyes wide-open, he studied the sky, amazed by the subtle change in colors as the sun disappeared below the western horizon. The soft blue hue changed to black velvet as the night dragged its heavy cloak across the land.

Struck by the simple beauty of the moment, he blinked misty eyes. Throughout his life, he'd seen many days wither away. One had always seemed like the other, nothing special or unusual. But since he'd accepted the Lord, simple things he'd always taken for granted had taken on new significance.

When he'd first opened the pages of the Bible he'd borrowed from Rebecca, the opening lines of Genesis had jumped out at him: In the beginning, God created the heavens and the earth. But it was nothing. Formless and dark. And then God said, "Let there be light." And the light shone out of the darkness.

It was the same way he felt inside. Spirit locked in darkness, he was hollow and frozen inside. He lived, but there was no life in him.

And then God had reached out to him. Offered the gift of salvation, Caleb watched his drab gray world morph into an array of bright colors. His heart had begun to beat again. The ice gripping his soul had thawed, giving him a new appreciation for life. The setting of the sun no longer signaled the end. It confirmed the awesome power of the Creator. Not only had God created light to warm the earth, but He had also given mankind a glimpse of the glory that awaited true believers. The knowledge was a gift.

Humbled and grateful, Caleb studied the endless depth of space. A sprinkle of stars glowed in the far distance.

Thank you for this day, Lord.

A sensation of peace washed over him. He no longer felt like he was running from his unhappy past. Now he looked forward to embracing the future. His arms were wide-open. He was ready to live and find someone to love.

Closing his eyes, he focused on his surroundings. The warmth of the day lingered on the gentle breeze. Insects buzzed over a variety of late-summer flowers blooming in the gardens. The sound of night birds and the whirring of cicadas added a lulling ambiance to the background.

Drawing in a breath, he took in the odors scenting the air. The smell of warm grass, saddle leather, livestock and damp earth were enhanced by the tang of the mesquite wood Levi had used for the cookout earlier in the evening. Taking advantage of the weather, the evening meal had been moved outside. On a grill made from natural stone, slabs of steak were laid over an open flame. The result was mouthwatering, barbecued beef with a distinct smoky flavor. Tender and flavorful, the meat was accompanied by grilled potatoes, corn on the cob and onions. Tall glasses of sweet tea washed it all down. Dessert was bread pudding loaded with chunks of apples and raisins, drizzled with homemade vanilla sauce.

Once supper was finished, Levi led the family through the evening's devotional. After a closing prayer of thanks, everyone drifted away to take care of the sundry chores that needed to be done before bed. Levi had gone to bed down the livestock for the night. Amity had turned her attention to her mending. Gail had her hands full with her toddler. Only Florene was absent, choosing to spend time with her *Englisch* boyfriend.

"You're quiet. Is everything all right?"

Jarred out of his doze, Caleb reluctantly opened his eyes. He turned his head toward the voice. Rebecca sat nearby tending to Matthew. Since his last feeding, the infant turned fussy, acting as if he were uncomfortable. Suspecting a tummy ache, Rebecca had turned to a natural remedy to ease his discomfort. Boiling chamomile, fresh ginger and peppermint into a strong brew, she'd given him a teaspoon of the liquid. Laying the infant on his back, she'd massaged his belly with a circular motion. The baby had drifted to sleep.

Struck by the serenity enveloping her, he couldn't help but stare. Framed in the fading light of day, she

"One Minute" Survey

You get up to **FOUR books** <u>and</u> a Mystery Gift...

YOU pick your books –
WE pay for everything.
You get up to FOUR new books and a Mystery Gift...
absolutely FREE!
Total retail value: Over $20!

Dear Reader,

Your opinions are important to us. So if you'll participate in our fast
and free "One Minute" Survey, YOU can pick up to four wonderful
books that WE pay for when you try the Harlequin Reader Service!

As a leading publisher of women's fiction, we'd love to hear from you.
That's why we promise to reward you for completing our survey.

IMPORTANT: Please complete the survey and return it. We'll send
your Free Books and a Free Mystery Gift right away. And we pay for
shipping and handling too! *We pay for*
← *EVERYTHING!*

Try **Love Inspired® Romance Larger-Prin**t and get 2 books and
fall in love with inspirational romances that take you on an uplifting
journey of faith, forgiveness and hope.

Try **Love Inspired® Suspense Larger-Pri**nt and get 2 books where
courage and optimism unite in stories of faith and love in the face of
danger.

Or TRY BOTH!

Thank you again for participating in our "One Minute" Survey. It
really takes just a minute (or less) to complete the survey… and your
free books and gift will be well worth it!

If you continue with your subscription, you can look forward to
curated monthly shipments of brand-new books from your selected
series, always at a discount off the cover price! Plus you can cancel
any time. So don't miss out, return your One Minute Survey today to
get your Free books.

Pam Powers

"One Minute" Survey

GET YOUR FREE BOOKS AND A FREE GIFT!

✓ Complete this Survey   ✓ Return this survey

▲ DETACH AND MAIL CARD TODAY! ▼

1 Do you try to find time to read every day?

☐ YES   ☐ NO

2 Do you prefer books which reflect Christian values?

☐ YES   ☐ NO

3 Do you enjoy having books delivered to your home?

☐ YES   ☐ NO

4 Do you share your favorite books with friends?

☐ YES   ☐ NO

YES! I have completed the above "One Minute" Survey. Please send me r
Free Books and a Free Mystery Gift (worth over $20 retail). I understand that I a
under no obligation to buy anything, as explained on the back of this card.

☐ **Love Inspired®
Romance
Larger-Print**
122/322 CTI G2AK

☐ **Love Inspired®
Suspense
Larger-Print**
107/307 CTI G2AK

☐ **BOTH**
122/322 & 107/307
CTI G2AL

FIRST NAME

LAST NAME

ADDRESS

APT.#

CITY

STATE/PROV.

ZIP/POSTAL CODE

EMAIL ☐ Please check this box if you would like to receive newsletters and promotional emails from
Harlequin Enterprises ULC and its affiliates. You can unsubscribe anytime.

Your Privacy—Your information is being collected by Harlequin Enterprises ULC, operating as Harlequin Reader Service. For
a complete summary of the information we collect, how we use this information and to whom it is disclosed, please visit
our privacy notice located at https://corporate.harlequin.com/privacy-notice. From time to time we may also exchange your
personal information with reputable third parties. If you wish to opt out of this sharing of your personal information, please
visit www.readerservice.com/consumerchoice or call 1-800-873-8635. Notice to California Residents—Under California
law, you have specific rights to control and access your data. For more information on these rights and how to exercise them,
visit https:// corporate.harlequin.com/california-privacy.

© 2023 HARLEQUIN ENTERPRISES ULC
™ and ® are trademarks owned by Harlequin Enterprises ULC. Printed in the U.S.A.

LI/LIS-1123-OM

BUSINESS REPLY MAIL
FIRST-CLASS MAIL   PERMIT NO. 717   BUFFALO, NY

POSTAGE WILL BE PAID BY ADDRESSEE

HARLEQUIN READER SERVICE
PO BOX 1341
BUFFALO NY 14240-8571

NO POSTAGE
NECESSARY
IF MAILED
IN THE
UNITED STATES

was more than pretty. Glowing with tenderness, she was beautiful. His breath stalling, a glimmering sensation circled through his stomach. She was close enough to touch, a desire he found hard to resist.

But he did nothing.

He was cognizant enough to realize she didn't feel the same way. The conversation they'd had earlier in the day had cut a deep track in his memory. Without being rude, she'd made it clear there was a subtle divide between them. Despite their attraction, both were expected to stay on their own side of the fence.

She isn't looking for a doctor with an existential identity crisis. Oh, and by the way, you're not Amish...

Disappointment stung. But focusing on rejection wouldn't do any good. Neither of them could change who they were. Or the rules that kept them apart.

Swallowing the lump blocking his throat, he forced a smile. "Everything's fine."

"You went so quiet. By the look on your face, you were a million miles away." Playfully tapping his forehead, she added, "I wonder what you were thinking."

Caleb turned away. "Oh, it was nothing. Just stupid things."

She laughed. "I'm sure it was more than that. Let me guess. You were thinking about the bright lights of Los Angeles and wondering how you ended up in a little cow town in the middle of nowhere."

He stared into the growing darkness. Solar-powered path lights had begun to pop on, lighting the way for those out after dark. The soft glow added to the ambiance of the evening. It was a moment of perfect peace, a little slice of heaven on earth.

"Actually, no. California's the furthest thing from my

mind." And it was. Now that he'd spent a few nights in a tiny town, the idea of living in a city congested with traffic held no appeal. He wasn't looking forward to joining the rat race again, elbowing others aside in pursuit of the almighty dollar.

Meeting the Lord had stopped him dead in his tracks. His priorities were shifting, pointing in other directions. There were so many new paths to follow. But which one was the right one? He wasn't sure. The only thing he did know what that he had a lot of praying to do.

She cocked her head, sending the strings of her *kapp* askew. "I'm glad to hear that. I like having you here."

"You do?" Encouraged, he shifted to a sitting position. He moved carefully, reluctant to disturb the sleeping infant nestled between them.

"We all do. I thank *Gott* you were here to help with Matthew. And I know Dr. Gordon's grateful, too."

"I've never met a more stubborn old mule. I think I offended him when I told him to stay off his feet. If he doesn't stay home and rest, he won't recover from another collapse."

"You can't blame him for being concerned about his patients. Since the last doctor quit, he's carried everything himself. It's not like the old days, when his *daed* practiced, too."

He shot her a look. "His father was a doctor?"

"Ja," she affirmed. "And so was his *grossdaadi*. The Gordons came from Amish, you know. Abner Gordon— that was his granddaddy's name, I believe—left the community when he was a young man and worked his way through medical school. Then he came back to Burr Oak and started the clinic. That was sometime in the thirties, I think."

"That's almost a century ago. And quite an accomplishment. Correct me if I'm wrong, but don't the Amish only go to the eighth grade?"

"It's all that is required. Most Amish don't believe they need to know more than reading, writing and basic math."

A low whistle slipped through his lips. "Imagine that. An Amish kid making it into medical school."

"I don't know if that would be possible nowadays," she conceded. "But back then people with knowledge of natural remedies were considered to be doctors of a sort."

Recalling the blend she'd used to soothe Matthew's upset tummy, he nodded. He'd always believed nature should be included in treatment options before turning to the prescription pad.

"That's what we call naturopathic medicine today."

"Dr. Gordon still relies on the old ways to treat patients, including prayer. His is a faith-based practice. People here know and trust him."

"I take it he has no sons to follow in his footsteps?"

"*Nein*. His *tochters* didn't go into medicine, nor did his *schwiegersohns*. As it is, he is the last."

"That's a shame."

"The last doctor left after a year. We'd all heard there was supposed to be a new fellow, but he seems to have backed out."

"That, I don't get. Most young doctors would jump at the chance."

Rebecca knotted her fingers together in her lap. "It's the location. And the compensation. The Gordon *familie* has always run the clinic as a ministry and not-for-profit, so it doesn't pay a lot. And many of Dr. Gordon's patients are rural folks with no health insurance. Not just the Amish, but *Englisch*, too. A lot of them don't have much, so they offer what they have instead."

"Oh? Like what?"

"Things like eggs, fresh produce or a slab of beef. Others might pay with a handmade quilt or other craft. Whether they can pay or not, Dr. Gordon never turns away anyone needing care."

"People pay in groceries?"

"*Ja.* Dr. Gordon recognizes that things like that have value, too."

"I suppose he eats well."

"It's common knowledge the money he does get keeps the lights on and pays his staff. For himself— Well, he's poor as a church mouse. But he says the Lord provides what he needs and that is enough."

Caleb lowered his gaze. The elderly physician hadn't strayed far from his roots. He lived simply and served his community with kindness and humility. His ministry was driven by a desire to heal.

Unfortunately, Caleb couldn't say the same for himself. He'd chosen medicine because he wanted the success and prestige his father had achieved. Jealously had seeded his heart. Reaping what he'd sown had turned him into a bitter, lonely man.

Accepting the gift of salvation had washed away his sins, freeing him from his inner demons. But going to his knees meant more than having a clean slate with heaven. It meant obeying and living in a way that would please God.

It was time to give back, to make a difference.

Trembling from the lesson the Lord had delivered, he bowed his head.

Don't talk the talk unless you can walk the walk.

Chapter Nine

The clinic opened at eight. Arriving a few minutes early, Caleb parked next to the cars belonging to employees.

Fighting a stomach full of knots, he blew out a breath. Today would be his first seeing patients outside of a hospital setting. As an EMS working in emergency medicine, his job was to diagnose and stabilize before sending the patient on to an attending physician. Working in a fast-paced environment where human lives hung in the balance meant he didn't have time to forge personal relationships with patients.

As a general practitioner, Dr. Gordon had the luxury of developing an ongoing relationship with his patients, providing continuity of care. Treating common medical conditions and performing routine exams usually was the extent of a small clinic's abilities.

Stepping into the older physician's shoes—even temporarily—was going to be a challenge. A bit on the gruff side, Caleb had never been associated with a personable bedside manner. Rushed for time, he was short and to the point. Determined to be better than his father, he'd let personal relationships fall to the wayside.

And while he got along with his coworkers, there were few he'd call friends.

Shaking his head, he dragged a hand across his face. Meeting Rebecca and her family had changed his entire outlook. He was no longer focused on himself or his own selfish wants and needs.

You were a jerk, Caleb. It's no wonder you ended up alone.

Shamed by his past behavior, he looked at the sky. It was time to grow up.

"I'll do better, Lord. Just bear with me."

Lowering his head, he sent up another quick prayer. When the day was done, he intended to spend some time on his knees. He'd been set straight, but God still had a lot of work to do. And while he knew that faith wouldn't instantly solve all his problems, it offered a solid foundation upon which to build a future.

A cheery voice followed a tap on the driver's side window. "Good morning, Doctor."

Eyes snapping open, Caleb caught sight of Karyn. Dressed in scrubs, with her purse tucked under one arm, she stepped back to allow him to open the door.

"Good morning." Locking the vehicle, he pocketed the keys. "I hope I'm not late."

Karyn smiled as they fell into step, walking side by side. "No, you're right on time." Reaching the staff entrance, she punched in the code that allowed entry into the building. "We were all wondering if you'd come."

Following her toward a small employee break room, Caleb spread his hands. "I made a deal to show up, so here I am."

Stowing her purse in a locker, Karyn clocked in. "And I'm grateful you did. To work here, you have to have the heart to help." She shook her head as she closed her locker. "Not a lot of people do nowadays."

"I'm here to do what I can. It isn't much, but I'll do my best."

"I'm actually glad it happened, to tell you the truth."

"Oh? Why?"

"Dr. Gordon hasn't been himself lately."

"In what way?"

"He seems more distracted. Forgetful." Karyn pursed her lips before continuing. "Most days he's fine, but then there are moments when he seems to have problems concentrating."

"That is a symptom of fatigue," he said. "But other issues might be at play."

"You don't think it's something worse?"

"Anything is possible. And it's certainly something I'll take note of. If nothing else, it might be time for him to take a cognitive assessment."

Relief lightened her expression. "Thank you, Doctor. I appreciate you listened to what I had to say."

Caleb nodded. He liked Karyn and found her to be competent and professional. When Dr. Gordon had momentarily blanked while weighing the newborn, she'd stepped in without missing a beat. By the way she'd handled the moment, it was clear she was accustomed to monitoring her employer. Her concerns were valid.

"You'd be remiss in your duties if you didn't report what you've witnessed."

"It's sad to see David in decline. He's done so much for our community. He'll be hard to replace when he does retire."

"I've no doubt of that."

Ending the conversation, she pointed toward a larger

locker. "I guess we should get to work. Lab coats are there. Should be one that'll fit you."

Caleb looked. Most were on the shabby side. But since he wasn't going to a fashion show it didn't matter. Finding one in his size, he slipped it on. Truth be told, he wasn't expecting to see many patients. By now word had probably gotten around that Dr. Gordon was off his feet for a while. Some folks might not cotton to seeing a new doctor, especially one who was temporary. People expected to know who was in the exam room.

Karyn made a motion with her head. "We've still got a few minutes before Renee unlocks the front door, so I'll show you around."

He shut the locker. "That'd be great."

They walked down a short hall.

"Some of it you've seen, so we'll pass that by. There are two additional exam rooms. We also have a med room—it's always locked, key code, of course. Most of what we have is for treating minor ailments. You already know we're not equipped for major emergencies. Those are sent on to Eastland."

Nodding as she talked and pointed, Caleb looked every which way. He'd suspected the clinic only had the bare necessities, and he was correct. Nothing was new, but it was certainly well used. The building was old, and the entire operation begged for an upgrade, including the computer used by the receptionist. The system looked to be at least ten years out of date. Only someone familiar with Dr. Gordon's archaic filing system would be able to work their way through the multitude of folders filling shelf after shelf.

Karyn opened one last door. "The doctor says you can use his office while he's away."

Caleb walked inside. "That's fine. I'll try not to bother anything."

The furnishings and decorations were sparse, as austere as the man who inhabited the space. A few tasteful prints were hung on the walls, as were a couple of plaques. "The best doctor gives the least medicine," read one. "Prayer is the best medicine," read another. Simple, wise words.

A look at the bookshelf revealed titles any physician would want to keep on hand, along with a selection addressing natural and holistic remedies. A Bible, a hymnal and a couple of Christian-themed books rounded out the collection. Manila folders were stacked on the desk. Labeled neatly, these were patient files.

Leaning against the door frame, Karyn eyed him from head to foot. A look of bemusement played around the corners of her mouth.

He glanced up. "Something wrong?"

"I'm thankful you're here. Dr. Gordon needed a break."

"I agree. He's overworked and needs to take it easy."

"I know he wants to." A frown pulled down the corners of her mouth. "I can't tell you how many hours Dr. Gordon spent on the phone trying to recruit new doctors."

"I've been told. I've also been told why. True?"

Karyn worried her lower lip, unsure if she should speak or not. "Yeah. It's the money," she admitted. "I'm afraid the clinic can't pay a lot."

Chuffing, he shook his head. "Gotcha." Having been through med school, he knew most residents were tired of cheap food and living in dumpy apartments by the time they graduated. Loaded with debt, many sought the highest-paying internships they could find. The competition was fierce to secure a good position.

He'd never had that problem. If he made the grades, his parents had paid his way. He'd never had to hustle, worry about how to make the rent or where his next meal was coming from.

Regret prodded hard. It was another blessing he'd overlooked. God had handed him every advantage and he'd failed to appreciate it. His resolve to do better strengthened.

"The thing is, they can make it here just fine," Karyn said, eager to talk through her frustration. "Rent and utilities are low, and a savvy shopper can go to the market and get all kinds of food fresh from the garden. And living among the Amish isn't so bad. They're good people, and fair to outsiders."

"Sounds like you've been there."

She nodded. "I have. I didn't want to move to the middle of nowhere just to make half the money."

"So why did you?"

"My kids." Rolling her eyes, she made a face. "My ex-husband left me right before I graduated. He kept the house and kicked us out. I had nothing but the clothes on my back, my children and a car. I didn't have a spare dime and I needed cheap—and I do mean cheap—rent. I thought Burr Oak would be awful."

"But?"

"It turns out my kids love it. The school district is small, but they get more attention from their teachers. They have their sports and friends and go to church. And they aren't out running the streets, hanging out with gangs or using drugs. We don't have a lot, but we don't need it to get by."

"Sounds like it worked out."

Her face lit up. "It was the best decision I ever made. One of the first things I learned from Dr. Gordon was that God will provide. I wasn't a real churchgoer when I moved here, but David kept sharing the Lord's word. The things he said sank in and I became a believer."

He grinned. "I have it on good authority that God can work miracles."

Karyn cocked her head. "Are you a Christian, Doctor?"

"I'm a new believer," he confessed. "I've recently accepted Christ as my savior."

"How wonderful for you! You are a new creation."

"I'm afraid I don't understand what that means. It's only been a little while and I've got a lot to learn."

She laughed. "You'll get there." Turning up her wrist, she looked at her watch. "Will you look at that? It's already ten past eight because I've stood here flapping my jaws." She bustled out of the office, heading toward the lobby.

Straightening his coat, Caleb followed.

The receptionist was busy arranging files and fielding phone calls. Doors unlocked, people trickled into the waiting room for their appointments.

Karyn scooped up a folder. "Guess we'd better get started." Calling a name, she escorted a woman and her child toward the exam rooms.

Hanging up the phone, Renee offered an apologetic smile. "Looks like you have a busy day ahead, Dr. Sutter. We're booked solid."

Sucking in a breath, Caleb selected a file. Nervous as a new intern on his first day, his hand shook more than a little...

* * *

The bench swing creaked when Rebecca sat down. Sighing with relief, she allowed herself to relax. The day had been a busy one and she was worn down. Pressing a hand against her forehead, she closed her eyes. Fussy and out of sorts, the *boppli* had kept her on her feet since the crack of dawn. As the day wound down, he'd finally settled into a doze. After arriving home from her shop, Amity had offered to watch him so Rebecca could take a break.

Grateful to catch a breath of fresh air, she sipped from a tall glass of iced lemonade. Not the artificial kind that came powdered in a jar but made from real lemons squeezed by hand. Fresh took more time, but the taste was well worth the extra effort. Sweetened with just a touch of sugar, the tang made the lips pucker just right.

Gazing across the front yard, she noted the sun had angled to the west, the beginning of its journey toward the far horizon. A light breeze winnowed through the trees, tempering the heat of the long afternoon. A flurry of dirt about a quarter of a mile down the road indicated the travel of a vehicle. Caleb's rental pulled to a stop a few minutes later.

He opened the door then stepped out. Seeing her, he offered a wave before bending back inside. The cargo van was a far cry from the sleek SUV he was accustomed to driving, but he hadn't complained about its size or bulk.

Tucking a few books beneath his arm, he walked up the stone path to join her. A white lab coat covered the simple outfit he'd worn to the clinic; a white shirt tucked into tan slacks and loafers. The barest trace of stubble darkened his cheeks and chin.

As she watched him closely, Rebecca's breath caught. There was no denying that Caleb was an attractive man. And she liked looking. She also found his gentle manner and intelligence beguiling.

Senses tingling, a daydream flittered through her mind. An image of Caleb dressed in a plain shirt and broadfall trousers with a pair of black suspenders filled her thoughts. The pleasure derived from the image warmed her.

"My, you look comfortable sitting there," he greeted. "Mind if I join you?"

Her picture-perfect fantasy shattered.

Scolding herself for her flight of fancy, Rebecca shook her head. Liking Caleb was perfectly innocent. But coveting him, wishing him to be something he was not, those weren't the kind of thoughts that were proper to entertain. Friendship was the most she could offer. It would have to be enough.

"Please do." She scooted over to make room.

He sat. "Ah, it feels good to get off my feet." Setting the books he carried between them, he stretched out his long legs.

She cocked her head. "Busy day?"

Running a hand through his hair, he nodded. "Standing room only." He blew out a breath. "I don't think I've seen that many patients in years."

"Oh? Correct me if I'm wrong, but you worked in an ER, right? Aren't those busy?"

He shook his head. "I worked the night shift and it's a little slower. Generally, there is a higher volume of patients during the day because it's a time when people are up and more active."

"How did you like working in the clinic?"

"It is different from working ER trauma. Here, I have the time to visit with patients and get to know them on a more personal level. It feels like I'm practicing medicine again and not just running people through an assembly line to keep them alive. In the ER, you might get a few minor cases of the common flu, but most patients come in with severe trauma. Car accidents, gunshots…things like that. The whole night can go from zero to sixty in seconds."

"I heard you tell Dr. Gordon you'd done it for a long time."

Impressed, he passed her a look. "Yeah. But even before Richard and Audrey died, it was getting to be a drag. If they'd lived, I think I still would have made the move. It was time for a change." Despite his cheerful manner, the shadows of sadness lingered in the depths of his eyes.

"Why California?"

"What's not to like?" He offered a cockeyed grin. A hint of mischief waltzed through his expression. "Sun. Surf. Blondes on the beach."

Rebecca arched a brow back at him. "You like blondes. *Gut* to know." Her own hair was a mousy shade of brown and rather dull.

He dropped the pretense. "Um, forget I said that last part. That's not the impression I meant to imply."

She raised a hand. "It's okay. I get what you're saying."

Sitting straighter, Caleb shook his head. "I didn't mean to say that I'm all about chasing women. I'm not. I meant it when I accepted the Lord. And in that acceptance, I know I need to change my ways. I intend to live to please God."

"I think that's admirable. But the Lord doesn't expect perfection overnight. He knows we will stumble. He knows we will fall. And that is why He gave us Jesus. Through His grace, we are forgiven."

"I guess that's true. But I am going to do better."

His sincerity warmed her. She believed him. Having suffered a tremendous loss, it only made sense he'd want to rebuild his life.

"What are your plans when you get to California?"

He laid a hand atop the books he'd carried in. The titles referenced the practice of general medicine. "Honestly, I don't know. I thought I had my mind made up. But I'm not so sure."

"Any reason in particular?"

"Actually, yes. I'm concerned Dr. Gordon may be sicker than he's letting on."

"Why would you think that?"

Frustration crinkled his brow. "Far be it from me to speak out of place, but Karyn mentioned a few concerns she has. If anyone would know, she would."

"Is there anything you can do?"

"I'm going to give Dr. Gordon a few more days to rest. I'll speak to him after the weekend. If I can't get any answers, I might have to take further steps."

"Like what?"

"Contact the state medical board."

Alarm filled her. "But what would happen if the board made Dr. Gordon step down?"

"Let's hope it doesn't come to that." Shaking his head, he let the subject trail off. "But enough about me. How was your day?"

Rebecca rolled her eyes. "Why, all about the *bop-*

pli." She exhaled with exasperation. "Diapers, feedings, crying and more diapers."

"Guess that's part of being a parent."

"It is exhausting. But I love it. Caring for *kinder* is a privilege. Not everyone gets to experience that joy."

Eyes twinkling, he wrinkled his nose. "Changing diapers doesn't sound joyful to me."

"It's part of what comes with *youngies*," she laughed. "But the *gut* outweighs the bad, by far. Every day brings something new. Watching a little one grow and learn is a miracle. I'm humbled *Gott* has given me the chance to experience it."

"I suppose you're right. I never learned to enjoy the small things."

"I try to stay positive. These last few years have been hard, but I can't keep letting the past get me down. *Gott* showed me another path."

"Sounds like you have quite a few plans for the future."

"I do. I'd planned to open a daycare. But after talking with Evan, I think Burr Oak needs a *familie* services center more. Perhaps if Mary had help, she would have wanted to keep Matthew."

He looked at her with admiration. "I think it would be a fine use of your talents. Have you thought about going to the city council? Maybe the council members could allocate some funds toward setting up a resource center."

She blinked. "Could they do something like that?"

"Of course. That's why you pay property taxes. There should be a general fund for community and human services."

"What would I have to do to find out?"

"The best thing to do would be to speak to the mayor."

Worry suddenly gnawed her insides. Having an idea was one thing. Proposing it to the city was a different matter.

Rebecca was out of her depth. After retiring from teaching, she'd expected to spend the rest of her life as Mrs. Noel Yoast. Married to the man she loved, she'd wanted nothing more than to raise their *youngies* as they grew old together. After their engagement ended, she'd tried to get her teaching job back. But the position had already been filled by Nevah Collins, who was a former student and a capable young lady in her own right.

"What would I say?"

"The same thing you and Sheriff Miller discussed the other day. Matter of fact, it probably wouldn't be a bad idea to take him with you. You might even take Matthew, just to show the mayor the need is there."

She brightened. Working to serve those most vulnerable would be her ministry.

"I'm sure Evan would be willing."

"Sounds like a plan." Leaning back, he used the heel of one foot to rock the swing. The gentle swaying motion was soothing. Comfortable. Gaze fixed on her face, the barest hint of a smile lingered around the edges of his fine mouth.

"What?"

"I was just thinking how you're not what I'd expected the typical Amish girl to be like."

"And what did you think the typical Amish girl would be like?"

"Oh, you know what I mean. Sitting in front of your spinning wheel making yarn or maybe churning butter or canning vegetables. Things like that."

Rebecca couldn't help laughing. "Believe it or not, we still do those things. And contrary to popular belief, they aren't simple at all. There's a talent for using a spinning wheel. I can't do it myself, but Amity is rather *gut*. She makes her own thread for tatting and creates beautiful lace."

He laughed. "I meant no offense."

"None taken."

"And I have no idea what tatting is. But I know you're not typical, at all."

Self-conscious, she pulled her gaze away from his. Doing so was the hardest thing she'd ever done. If she'd had her way, she would be content to sit and look into his stormy gray eyes for hours.

Rattled by the thought, she clasped her hands in her lap. "You are too generous with your praise. *Gott* willing, I'll do some *gut* in this world."

Caleb reached for her hand. Strong fingers closed around hers. His warm touch offered encouragement. "You can do anything you set your mind to, Rebecca. I believe that. I believe in you."

The conversation fell into a lull. They sat in silence, enjoying each other's company.

Gail poked her head out. "I thought I heard you pull up," she said, wiping her hands on a dishrag. "I've got fresh lemonade if you'd like some, Caleb."

He smiled graciously. "I'm good, thanks."

Gail nodded. "I'll have supper on the table in about a half hour."

She was about to go back inside when a pickup truck zipped up the gravel lane. The driver hit the brakes hard, sending a spray of dirt and rocks into the air. As the dust cleared, two people could be seen inside. Shouting and waving, the occupants were engaged in an argument. The passenger side door flew open.

Florene tumbled out. "Just leave me alone, Zane!" Crying hysterically, she slammed the door shut.

The driver buzzed the window down, tossing her phone after her. "Next time it'll be worse!" Slamming the massive vehicle into reverse, he peeled out of the drive. Roaring back down the road, he disappeared back onto the highway.

Watching him go, Florene crumpled to the ground.

Chapter Ten

Eyes widening, Rebecca jumped to her feet. "My *Gott*, what's happened?"

Shifting into emergency mode, Caleb was two steps ahead. "Let me get her." Crossing through the front yard, he hurried to Florene's side. He swooped her up in his arms, then carried her into the house.

Rebecca followed on his heels. Gail was close behind. The two of them watched as Caleb laid her on the sofa.

Florene tried to cover her face with her hands. "Just leave me alone!" she grated, attempting to stand.

Pressing a hand to her shoulder, Caleb gently pushed her back down. "Let me see your face."

Florene's body shook. "No," she mumbled. "I'm okay."

"Florene, let Caleb look at you." Face dead white, Gail pressed a hand to her protruding stomach. "I'm not of any mind to put up with your antics."

Fearing the worry would stress Gail, Rebecca circled an arm around her shoulders. "Calm down. It's going to be okay."

Gail burst into tears. "I'm so tired of the drama. All she and Zane do is fight."

Drawn out of the nursery, Amity walked into the living room. Matthew was cradled protectively in her arms. Toddling behind her, Sammy clutched her skirts to keep his balance. "What's going on?"

Rebecca cut her youngest sibling a look. It wasn't the first time Florene had come home emotionally wrought. Her drama had become a point of contention, and no amount of begging, pleading or prayer would have her see reason.

"She's been fighting with Zane again."

Amity's face turned into a frown. "I never liked him."

Rebecca pursed her lips, desperate to understand the attraction. A chill circled her spine. She'd suspected Zane was bad news. Now, she knew it.

Since starting her *rumspringa*, Florene had fallen in with the wrong crowd. She'd recently taken up smoking and had come home reeking of alcohol more than once. The source of her destructive behavior could be narrowed down to one culprit. An *Englischer*, Zane Robbins fancied himself a local hotshot. Driving a big truck, he flashed a lot of cash, both of which were rumored to come from drug money. Zane had puppy-brown eyes under a mop of blond hair that perfectly complemented his tanned physique. Having led a sheltered life until she was old enough to make her own choices, Florene wasn't emotionally equipped to resist the fast lifestyle he'd introduced her to.

Unwilling to take no for an answer, Caleb focused his gaze on Florene's bare arms. "I can see the bruises where he grabbed you. You want to show me what he did to your face?"

Bursting into sobs, Florene slowly lowered her hands. Her left cheek swelled with a large purple bruise.

Rebecca's hand flew to her mouth in horror. She'd feared something like this was going to happen. Zane had a temper and she'd known it was just a matter of time before he let his anger get the best of him.

Seeing her injuries, Caleb pressed his lips together. Tiny lines of dismay formed around his eyes. "How many times did he hit you?"

Florene dropped her head. "Just once." She ran a hand up one bare arm. The imprint of his fingers was etched into her skin. "Mostly he shook me."

"Has it happened before?"

Florene hesitated.

"Go on," Amity prodded. "Don't lie about it."

"A couple of times," Florene mumbled. "But Zane always says he's sorry and won't do it again."

A shiver slithered down Rebecca's spine. It horrified her to hear Florene admit previous abuse. But it also made sense. Time and again, her younger sister had taken to wearing long sleeves and heavy cosmetics. The realization sickened her to the core. A throb pulsed in her temple even as a wave of nausea threatened to overwhelm her.

She's been hiding the abuse.

Rebelling against her Amish upbringing, Florene didn't recognize the dangerous path she was walking. The partying. The drinking, The bad relationship. If she didn't stop now, she'd crash and burn. And when that happened, there would be no walking away.

Drawn by the commotion outside, Levi stormed through the back door. Seth hurried behind him.

"Why was Zane tearing down the road?" he demanded behind an angry scowl. "He spooked the horses we were riding and nearly got Seth thrown."

Gail hurried to calm her angry spouse. "Florene and Zane had another fight." Voice shaking, she added, "He hit her."

Levi's mouth went tight. "That's not acceptable. Me and that boy are going to have a little talk. I'm going to find him and we're going to settle this. Right now." Hat in hand, he turned to head back outside.

Gail grabbed his arm. "Levi, no! I don't want you going after Zane. He's too wild and settling things with your fists isn't the way to handle this."

Levi jerked away. "Someone his own size needs to teach him to mind his manners."

Gail gave a pleading look "*Nein*. That's not the Amish way, and you know it. When you came back to the church you promised to put your rough ways behind you. This isn't the rodeo. I know cowboys think they have to handle things with their fists, but you're better than that now. Going after Zane would only lead to more trouble we don't need."

Levi reluctantly backed off. "You're right, honey. I'll do what *Gott* says. We are to have nothing to do with a person who stirs up division." He looked to Florene. "Zane is no longer allowed on this property. I don't want you seeing him again."

Florene leaped to her feet. "That's not fair! I love him. He's asked me to marry him and we're planning to move in together."

Everyone looked at her in shock.

A prickling sensation crawled through Rebecca, settling like a stone in her lungs. "You can't be serious."

Florene shot a defiant look. "Well, I am. And there's nothing you all can do to stop me. I'm of age and I can make my own choices."

Levi nailed the errant girl with a frown. "If you're planning to marry Zane, you'd better pack your bags and leave."

Florene jumped to her feet. "I just might do that! You're not my *daed*, Levi. You don't tell me what to do!"

Gail visibly stiffened. "You will not talk to my *ehmann* like that. We have rules in this *haus*. If you choose not to live by them, you can go."

Florene's face took on a defiant scowl. "Fine. I'll pack."

Much to everyone's surprise, Caleb stepped in front of Florene as she tried to leave. "You'd be making a mistake if you move in with Zane," he said, speaking in an even voice. "Once an abuser starts hitting, it doesn't stop. It only gets worse."

Florene's hands shot out, smacking Caleb's chest. "You don't even know him! Most of the time he's a good guy."

Using his size as leverage, Caleb didn't flinch or raise a hand. "But what about the times he isn't?"

Florene backed off. "I—I don't understand."

Caleb didn't break his eye lock. "Go look in the mirror and you will see what I've seen thousands of times. A bruised woman who insists her boyfriend is *a good guy*. And then one day, he isn't. One day she doesn't come through the ER. One day they're wheeling her body into the morgue because that *good guy* went a little too far. Today, you're just a little bruised. What if he had choked you? Or hit you with something harder than his fist?"

Giving a frightened look, Florene shrank back. A shiver threatened her calm. Sitting back down, she wrapped her arms around her body. "But Zane says he loves me."

Caleb dropped to a knee in front of her. "Listen to me, and know I am speaking from experience. Any man who hurts a woman doesn't love her."

Lower lip trembling, tears spilled from Florene's eyes. "I don't understand why Zane acts that way. I was just texting a friend, and he blew up. He accused me of cheating on him. I'm not, but he always thinks I am."

"He wants to make you afraid. That's not love. It's control. And it's dangerous."

Wanting to back up Caleb's warning, Rebecca sat down. "You need to listen to the doctor." She wrapped an arm around Florene's trembling shoulders. "Caleb's worked in an emergency room. He knows what he's talking about."

Swooping up her toddler, Gail held Sammy protectively in her arms. "You need to break up with Zane. I don't want my *kinder* exposed to that kind of person."

Caleb stood. "You should file a report with Sheriff Miller. He'll arrest Zane for domestic abuse. A few days in jail might give him some time to think."

Eyes going wide, Florene shook her head. "No, I couldn't."

Rebecca hastened to explain. "Plain folks rarely involve the police in things like this. It's best to let the bishop handle problems in our community."

Caleb shook his head. "I'm not clear on that point of view. But since Zane isn't Amish, Sheriff Miller would be in a better position to deal with him."

"I agree," Levi said, stepping in. "Zane isn't Amish. It's only fitting *Englisch* law should deal with him."

Still holding Matthew, Amity chimed in. "If he's hit

you, he'll hit other girls, too. It's only right you do what you can to stop that."

Florene suddenly crumbled. *"Ja,"* she admitted, swiping at her eyes. "His temper's bad. I don't want anyone else to get hurt."

Levi set his hat back on his head. "Then it's settled. We'll go now. I'll get Ezra to drive us into town."

Sitting in the nursery, Caleb gently rocked Matthew. Needing a moment to step back and decompress, he'd offered to take care of the baby while Florene's family dealt with her crisis.

Though he'd never spent a lot of time around children, he found he enjoyed tending to the needs of a little one. Changing diapers wasn't a bother. And when Rebecca had insisted on buying the infant a few outfits, he'd been the one to whip out his credit card to pay for the items.

At peace just to sit and rock, he gazed at the infant's face. The little boy slept without a care in the world. Inconvenience had turned into the most wonderful experience of his life.

Don't know what happened. But I took the bait.

Hook, line and sinker.

He wanted to be a husband. And a dad.

A frown tugged his mouth down. Kind of hard to do since he didn't have a wife. Or a girlfriend.

The women he'd dated drifted back through his mind. He'd liked a lot of them, but there'd never been any spark. And even though his adoptive parents often reminded him he was nearing forty and needed to get a move on, he had no intention of settling. Maybe he was being too fussy, but he desired a levelheaded woman who wanted to stay home and raise their children. His mother was a dedicated career woman. She'd worked long hours and let housekeepers and nannies do her mothering. That wasn't what he wanted for his own offspring. He wanted his little ones to have a hands-on mom. Maybe he was being foolish, but he liked the glimpse he'd gotten into Amish ways. Family and children were the center of their lives.

His thoughts turned back to Rebecca. He never thought he'd meet *the one*. Even though she was eleven years younger than himself, he didn't feel it was an impossible age gap. Knowing she had fertility issues didn't bother him. There were treatments for her condition. And if those were unsuccessful, there was always the option of fostering.

Or we could adopt...

His mind circling toward another track, Caleb's throat tightened. Now that he knew he was adopted, he understood why he'd always felt like a square peg trying to fit into a round hole. The accident had opened his eyes to a whole new world. One he longed to embrace as his own.

A light tap sounded at the door. Rebecca stepped into the room. "I just wanted to let you know we're back."

Caleb stopped rocking. "How'd it go?"

"Florene filed a complaint against Zane." Relief crept through her expression. "He won't be coming around again."

"I trust Sheriff Miller can handle the matter."

"Evan's a *gut* friend. He's helped us through..." She paused, measuring her words. "Difficult times in the past."

"Did you have a chance to speak with him about meeting with the mayor?"

"*Ja*. He usually sees Mayor Andrews on Friday afternoons. He says he will take me with him." Crossing to the changing table, she busied herself arranging baby items. Strength and determination adorned her. "I forgot to say that Evan sent his thanks to you for talking to Florene."

"I hope no one's upset I put my two cents in. I know it wasn't any of my business."

"We are all grateful you were here to speak to her." Her hands trembled a little as she arranged and then rearranged the items. "We've been on her for months to drop Zane. But the more we spoke against him, the more she wanted to be with him. I think your warning helped open her eyes."

"I hate to say it, but I've seen that kind of abuse more than I care to admit. Didn't think I'd see it in the Amish community, though."

A bitter look twisted her expression. "Florene learned a hard lesson, I'm afraid. Thank *Gott* Zane didn't do more than shake her up. It could have been worse."

"I've never understood why girls like bad boys."

"Florene didn't start rebelling until our *daed* passed." She glanced toward him, sadness deepening her frown. "I can understand if she doesn't want to stay in the Plain community. But she's making such bad choices. I fear things won't end well for her."

"She's blessed to have people who care. A lot of folks don't have anyone to set them straight when they make wrong choices."

"Florene's as stubborn as an old laying hen." Her delicate hands clenched. "In my mind, we should keep to our own kind. She would do well to come back to the church, get baptized and find a *gut* Amish man."

"Can't say I don't agree." Now that he'd become a man of belief, he'd begun to recognize the corruption and decay plaguing *Englisch* society. The more he looked at it, the less he liked it.

The swaddled infant in his arms stirred then but didn't wake. Careful not to disturb the baby's sleep, he rose and tucked Matthew into his bassinet.

"You're so gentle with him. You would make a *gut daed.*"

The foreign words brushed against Caleb's ears. By now he understood several and could follow along in a rudimentary way when they'd switched to the *Deitsch.*

"I'd like to have kids. Someday."

Her eyes sparkled. "Any idea who their *mamm* will be?"

Stomach twisting with emotion, Caleb dropped his gaze. The feelings of attraction were all so new. As was the yearning for companionship. He longed for the love and acceptance of one special person.

Rebecca.

Shoving his hands in his pockets, he pretended to keep an eye on Matthew. He hoped she couldn't hear the pounding of his heart. Or see the longing in his eyes.

It was foolish even to consider the notion they could be together. She was Amish and wanted nothing to do with his world. And he didn't blame her one bit. Now that he'd lived among them, the Amish didn't seem so foreign. He didn't know why, but he felt right at home.

Turning his head, Caleb stared out the window. Pain rose in his chest, circling and squeezing his heart. The feelings of loneliness invaded him all over again. He was eager for a purpose, a guide that would help him understand who he really was? The feeling of living his life in some sort of perpetual limbo was unnerving and maddening.

He swallowed down the dryness plaguing his throat. *Would he ever belong anywhere?*

Chapter Eleven

"I'm sorry, Rebecca." Mayor Andrews shook his head sorrowfully. "As much as I hate to, I have to reject your proposal."

Listening to the decision, Rebecca felt an incongruous ripple of anger. She'd spent more than hour in the mayor's office, laying out her idea to open a resource for low-income mothers and their babies. She'd labored for days, laying out in writing the reasons such an establishment would benefit the community.

Close to snapping, she tempered her tongue. "But why not? I've given you a *gut* example and you have the temerity to say no. Mary Reese's story is just one of many. Why can't we extend a hand to help women like her?"

Hat in his lap, Sheriff Miller leaned forward. "I'd certainly like to hear the reasons myself, John. From what I heard, she's outlined a good plan to provide a much-needed service to unwed mothers and their babies in Burr Oak. Surely the city can offer a grant of some sort to help get it off the ground."

Seated behind his desk, the mayor offered a look of sympathy. A big, broad, dark-haired man, he was untidy and awkward in his manner and dress. Yet he was also an accountant in his professional life. He knew how to balance the books and stretch a dollar. The town had seen many improvements under his watch, all without raising taxes on the citizens. An honest man who'd never told a single untruth, he'd just been elected to his second term as mayor.

"I appreciate the support you're offering, Evan. And I will not argue about the need for more social service programs. But as good as the idea sounds on paper, there are multiple reasons the city can't move forward."

Rebecca forced herself to calm. Shifting to a more comfortable position, she gently rocked Matthew, who was cozy and safe in his travel seat. She'd wanted the mayor to see for himself the face of a child in need.

"And they are?" she demanded, unwilling to let him off the hook.

"I'm afraid the money just isn't there," the mayor said. "We're running on a thin budget as it is. We just don't have the discretionary funds to work with."

"What if we set it up as a charity and ask the public for donations?" Sheriff Miller asked.

"Assuming you intend this to be a charitable organization, you're going to have to come up with a reasonable plan to do business," the mayor explained. "What is your source of income? How will you pay qualified staff? Are you prepared to incorporate your charity with the state? You'll also need to file for tax-exempt status with the IRS." His narrow face twisted in a grimace of compassion. "I could go on, but you get what I'm saying."

Rebecca's lower lip trembled. Biting down, she attempted to control her emotions. She believed *Gott* had called her to do the work. Yet she felt helpless and over-whelmed, swimming against a strong tide that insisted on pulling her back into deep water. She was struggling to stay afloat, while other forces insisted on yanking her under.

"I had no idea it would take so much."

"Bureaucracy and red tape always tie things up. That's just the way government works." He offered a sympathetic look. "Don't get me wrong. I'm sympathetic to Matthew's story. But I believe what you're proposing is a lot larger than the resources you could reasonably gather."

Heart dropping to her feet, Rebecca gave him a pleading look. "Then where are mothers like Mary Reese supposed to go for help?"

Mayor Andrews sighed. "I hate being the big bad wolf, but you must understand my position. I have to look at putting the city funds where they will help the most. I don't know if you're aware of it, but we're facing a crisis as it is with the medical clinic."

Sheriff Miller's gaze sharpened. "I don't suppose this has anything to do with Dr. Gordon's collapse a few days ago?"

"It does," Andrews affirmed. "I received a call from David's wife—just this morning. She's let me know he intends to retire within the next few months."

"I didn't think he'd ever considered it," Sheriff Miller returned. "Always thought they'd have to take him out feet first."

Mayor Andrew's mouth flattened. "The choice was not his," he said in his blunt manner. "His health has taken a turn for the worse."

Stunned, Rebecca pressed her hands to her mouth.

Not two days ago Caleb had mentioned Dr. Gordon might be having medical issues. Now, it was confirmed.

"How terrible for him and his *familie*."

"We're going to have to face some hard facts. Once David Gordon retires, Burr Oak won't have a physician. No MD, no clinic."

"But the hospital in Eastland is almost a hundred miles away," she said.

"That's a hard trip for a lot of folks to make, especially for nonemergency care," Sheriff Miller added. "What if they are elderly or don't drive?"

Mayor Andrews raised his hands. "Please, you're preaching to the choir. I know it's an issue and I'm doing everything in my power to solve it."

"Can anything be done?" she asked, distressed by the grim revelation.

"I'm hoping by increasing the clinic's budget that we can bring in a new physician."

"Have you thought about making an offer to Caleb Sutter?" Sheriff Miller asked. "He's been filling in while David's off his feet. Word around is folks like him."

"Matter of fact, I have considered speaking with him," Andrews affirmed. "I did a little digging into his background, and he'd be an asset to our community. The hospital where he worked is gnashing its teeth over losing him. Word is he's heading into private practice in California—and they are going pay him the big bucks. I'm doing my best to come up with an amount he might find acceptable."

"How much?" Sheriff Miller asked.

"I'm not in a position to say," Andrews returned. "I'm crunching the numbers to try and make a decent offer."

Rebecca struggled to hold her composure. This was a U-turn she hadn't expected. As far as she was aware, Caleb's plans to go on to Los Angeles soon hadn't changed.

"Do you think he will accept?"

"I'm praying he'll say yes," Andrews said, pressing his palms together. "If someone isn't found to take over the clinic, everyone who needs medical care will suffer. It's not just locals we have to think about, but folks who live outside city limits—like your family does."

Memory prodded, she swallowed hard. A few months ago, Gail had had to rush Sammy into town for treatment. The *boi* had developed an earache and no home remedy had eased his discomfort. A trip to the clinic had uncovered the mystery. A bug had flown into Sammy's ear while he'd played outside. Removing the insect would have proved impossible in a home setting. Had it remained, it might have festered, causing a terrible infection.

Lowering her gaze, she looked at Matthew. Dr. Gordon also was providing Gail's prenatal care. While it was customary for Amish mothers to have their *youngies* at home with the help of an experienced midwife, there were times when things went wrong. Dr. Gordon had handled many births in his time, but he'd reached a point where he was no longer able to function competently. Caleb had extensive training in emergency medicine. Thanks to his knowledge and quick action, Mary Reese delivered her baby without having to be transported to a larger facility. The delay of a hundred miles could have meant the difference between life and death for both. Elderly and ill, the time had come for the old man to lay aside his burden.

"I think it's a good call, John," Sheriff Miller said. "We couldn't ask for a better candidate."

Mayor Andrews nodded. "I agree. I'm going to make this happen, even if I have to twist every arm of every council member. The only hope to save the clinic might be Dr. Sutter."

"By the look on your face, I take it the meeting didn't go well?"

Shaking her head, Rebecca scooped Matthew out of his car seat. *"Nein."*

Closing the oven, Gail straightened. The aroma of her baking filled the kitchen with the delicious scent of cinnamon and apples. Her white apron was spotted with flecks of flour, cinnamon and butter.

"That doesn't tell me much." Setting aside the potholder, she brushed smudges of flour off her cheeks and chin. "Care to explain?"

Rebecca flashed a tight-lipped smile. No matter how tidy she tried to be, Gail always looked as if she'd been run through the wringer and hung out to dry. Bun uncurling, long strands of hair had worked their way out from under her *kapp*. Levi always claimed his wife fixed her hair with the eggbeater.

"The mayor said the money isn't there to fund any sort of social services." Settling Matthew in his cradle swing, she claimed a spot at the table. Soothed by the gentle motion, the *boppli* drifted back to sleep.

Glancing toward her sleeping *youngie*, Gail set a kettle on the stove. Sammy slept in his playpen, thumb popped into his mouth, worn out by an afternoon of hard play.

"I can't imagine what would be more important than needy women and their *youngies*," she said, setting out two cups as the water heated. "But I suppose the mayor knows what he's doing."

Rebecca shook her head. Failure clutched her insides. She had so many plans. But the doors kept slamming in her face. Hopes dashed against the rock of disappointment, she struggled to put things into perspective. "Honestly, I knew he'd probably say no, but it didn't hurt to ask."

Gail went quiet, seeming to gather her thoughts. "I'm surprised to hear those words come out of your mouth," she said after a moment. "You usually try to knock down the wall when someone says you can't do something."

Rebecca sighed. Normally, that's just exactly what she'd do. But this wasn't any sort of circumstance where sheer grit and determination would help her gain an advantage.

"After the mayor explained the other projects he'd like to direct the money toward, I was inclined to agree." At this point, it wasn't her place to share what she'd learned.

The kettle whistled, sending a spew of steam into the air. Filling two cups with tea, Gail delivered them to the table. "I suppose he didn't leave you much room to argue."

"Nein."

"What will you do now?"

Rebecca gazed into her drink. It looked fathomless and offered no easy answers. "I don't know."

Gail smiled. Her expression revealed she had something important to say. "I do."

Adding a spoonful of sugar to her cup and stirring, she nodded. The scent of bergamot tickled her nostrils. "Then you know something I don't."

"The mayor might have said no to your social center, but you can still serve the community in a smaller way."

"Oh? How?"

Sipping her tea, Gail lowered her cup. "Create care packages for new mothers. Put together clothes, diapers, bottles…things like that. You could call it a *boppli bank*."

Her heavy mood lightened. If nothing else, Amish women were crafty. Many made baby clothes and other items to sell in the local market. She knew at least a dozen who would contribute without hesitation. Amity, too, made lovely things and could knit booties and cute little hats in the blink of an eye.

"That's not a bad idea."

"You could even ask Bishop Harrison to share the word about your project. I bet he'd even let you use the community center a few days a week. It has storage and office space."

The day's disappointment faded as excitement kicked in. The Bible stated that being faithful in little things would make a soul faithful in larger ones. A plant could not grow and blossom on its own. A seed had to be planted, nurtured and encouraged to grow. *Gott* had put in her heart a desire to help. And her ability to handle the small things would determine her ability to handle the big things.

Lowering her head, she sent up a silent prayer of thanks. Once again, the Lord had taken the boulder impeding her path and turned it into a pebble.

"I think it's a wonderful idea." Confidence returning, she added, "I'll speak to Bishop Harrison as soon as I can. I'm sure he'll like the idea as much as I do."

Gail had no chance to reply. The back door swung

open. Levi, Seth, Amity and Florene all crowded in at once. For once, Florene looked like the rest of them. She'd returned to wearing her Amish clothes, and the bruise on her face had faded after a few days of healing.

Rebecca glanced out the nearby window. The entire afternoon had slipped away. The sun was beginning to sink into the west. On Friday evenings, most everyone was home by five. After a hard week, people were ready to relax. To help raise funds for charity projects, the church hosted a bazaar at the community center. Board and card games would be set up, as well as a sing-along and other fun activities. A variety of desserts would also be served. Open to the community, it was a chance for Amish and *Englisch* to mingle.

Levi hung his hat on a peg by the door. "I'm so glad it's Friday." Dusty and hot, the scent of leather and manure clung to his clothes. Seth, too, reeked of the cattle pens.

Gail ruefully surveyed her floor. "Boots off, please."

Bending, Levi complied. "Sorry." Straightening, he grinned and pulled his wife in for a kiss on the cheek.

Gail wrinkled her nose. "You're filthy." Giving a mock frown, she shooed him back. "Take your stinking self upstairs and bathe." Hands going to her hips, she added, "You, too Seth."

Seth bobbed his head. "Yes, ma'am."

Both trooped off to wash. As they passed through the living room, Sammy woke from his nap. Seeing his father and big *bruder*, he eagerly climbed to his feet.

"Da me!" he cried and held out his arms.

Levi scooped up the little *boi*. "I'll change him," he called before heading up the stairs.

"Put him in his blue pant set," Gail answered back.

"Will do."

Laying aside her purse, Amity bent over Matthew. "How is the little one today?" Vivacious and engaging, she glowed with the good cheer that made her an effective saleswoman. Her venture into retail netted her a nice living. Having outgrown the booth she rented—first at the farmer's market and then the mall—she was searching for a larger retail space to purchase.

"He's been the perfect angel."

Standing in silence, Florene sniffed the air. "Far be it from me to say anything, but I think something's burning."

Gail's eyes widened. "*Ach*, I forgot my baking!" Grabbing a mitt, she threw open the oven door. A plume of smoke rose over two blackened pies. Fishing them out, she placed them on a rack to cool.

Florene snickered. "Won't be selling those tonight."

"You don't have to be mean about it." Pressing a hand against her forehead, Gail frowned at the ruined dessert.

Puffing up like a tiny adder, Amity gave Florene a poke. "That's enough."

"Ouch!" Florene rubbed her side. "Why'd you do that?"

"Why do you always have to make fun of people?" Amity scolded. "Instead of laughing, why don't you offer a hand?"

Gail dumped the burned pies in the trash. "I don't have time to bake fresh ones. I'll simply have to go empty-handed. I'll just donate what they would have sold for."

Embarrassed to be called out, Florene fidgeted. "I can make some five-minute fudge, and fancy it up with chopped pecans. It'll only take an hour to set in the icebox. Then I can cut it into squares and wrap it up pretty. And if you have any dough and apples left, I can make some fried apple pies, too."

Gail brightened. "Would you?"

"I'll just have enough time." Walking to the cabinets, Florene took down the pots she would need before fetching the ingredients.

Amity smiled. "That's better. *Familie* should work together."

The rev of a vehicle pulling into the drive was followed by the sound of a door slamming. A polite knock at the back door followed.

"Caleb," Gail scolded. "Why are you still knocking? As long as you're staying here, you might as well just come on in."

Face breaking into a shy smile, he shrugged off the lab coat he'd taken to wearing since starting at the clinic. "It feels rude to just walk in."

"As long as you are staying here, you are part of the *familie.*"

"We wouldn't have it any other way," Amity said.

His eyes crinkled at the corners as he took in the cozy kitchen and living room. "I have to admit it's starting to feel like home. Keep spoiling me and I'll never want to leave."

"Home is where the heart is," Gail quipped back.

"Someday I'll have one of my own." Laughing, he beelined toward Matthew. Frame lean and strong, he walked with an easy, limber grace. "And how is our little one today?" Awakened by the commotion, the *boppli* stared up at him.

Watching Caleb interact with Matthew, Rebecca felt warmth suffuse her throat. *Our little one.* How lovely the words sounded. Both had captured her heart in different ways, but together they were an unbeatable combination. She longed to gather them in her arms, hold on tight and never let them go.

Suppressing a sigh, she tucked the precious image away. The vision of them as a happy *familie* existed only in her imagination.

"He's fit as a fiddle. And has the lungs to prove it."

"That's just what I wanted to hear." Caleb scooped up the infant. "I sure did miss you, sport."

Delighted, Matthew cooed back, kicking his arms and legs with glee. Checked every morning, he was making excellent progress. Barely a week old, he'd already gained a few ounces. Monitoring his heart murmur, Caleb had found no further cause for concern. Mary's little one was healthy and on track to meet all his developmental milestones.

Rebecca's stomach did a slow backflip. The sight was heartwarming. Through the time she'd spent with Caleb, her fondness for him had grown stronger. Watching him grow as a Christian was an honor and a delight. After a long day at the clinic, he eagerly joined in the evening devotional. Embracing *Gott*, he spoke of the changes he wanted to make in his life. Finding a place, settling down and building a future where he could serve the Lord was on his mind.

Watching him with Matthew, she recalled what she'd said the night he arrived. Though he might believe otherwise, the accident that had stranded him was no accident after all. She didn't know how she knew. She just did.

As if reading her mind, he raised his gaze. His eyes locked with hers, but not in an intrusive way. A grin stretched his mouth. Genuinely enthralled with Matthew, he was reaching out to share the moment.

Breath stalling, Rebecca turned her head. There was a connection between them, a tangible thing she could almost reach out and touch. The bond they'd developed while caring for the *boppli* was undeniable.

A shiver circled her spine as the mayor's dire prediction came back to haunt her. The emergency the town faced preyed on her mind. Goose bumps spread across her bare skin even as emotion stole her ability to breathe.

Caleb couldn't leave. Burr Oak needed him. Desperately.

Chapter Twelve

The church bazaar started at seven and would run through the evening. Eager to socialize, folks had turned out to devour the home-baked desserts, play games and share a bit of gossip. Packed full, the community center was warm and inviting.

Enjoying the pleasant gathering, Celeb looked around. After working at the clinic for the past few days, it was a nice chance to explore the community in a social setting. More than a few faces were familiar, and he was gratified to be greeted with smiles, waves and even a few handshakes. The acceptance helped calm his nerves. People knew him. He wasn't just another face in the crowd.

"Would you like to try some zucchini bread?" a woman working the dessert table asked.

"Or maybe a piece of Shoofly pie?" another said behind a cheerful smile.

Eyeing the selections, Caleb had a hard time deciding what to choose. Everything looked delicious.

Overwhelmed, he turned to Levi. "Which would you recommend?"

Levi laughed. "I have a hard time picking myself." He pointed. "But I never turn down a chance to have a slice of Alva Trotter's carrot cake. She puts in real bits of carrots, walnuts and pineapple. It's the best I've ever had."

Standing nearby, Sheriff Miller also browsed the desserts. Dressed in casual clothing, he was off duty. His clothes weren't unlike those worn by other Amish men; dark trousers, a white shirt and black boots. Hair slicked back and clean-shaven, a straw hat dangled from his hand.

"I always have a hankering for Lara Caster's cinnamon-applesauce bread," he said.

Caleb glanced at the lanky man. He liked the sheriff and was glad he'd supported Rebecca on her bid to get city funding for her social center. Getting turned down had disappointed her, but it hadn't stopped her plans.

"I'll have the carrot cake, too."

The women smiled and nodded, slicing and serving with quiet efficiency. "Enjoy your dessert," one said, holding out a paper plate. There was also a selection of beverages, ranging from milk for *youngies* to soft drinks and coffee for the older folks. As the public had paid at the door to enter, there was no awkward exchange of money. There was no set price to enter. People paid what they could comfortably afford to give.

Ready to eat, the men made their way to an empty table. After they'd arrived, the women had scattered into the crowd, eager to visit with friends. Seth had disappeared to join other boys his age. Still caught in her boyfriend drama, Florene had elected to stay home.

"I don't know how my middle's going to handle this," Sheriff Miller said wryly, digging into his food. "All I do nowadays is sit behind a desk pushing a pencil."

Levi forked up a bite of cake. "Come on out to the ranch and wrangle some of those Longhorns for a day. You'll sweat if off working in that hot sun."

Sheriff Miller laughed. "I just might do that sometime." Swallowing, he looked to Caleb. "How do you like Burr Oak, Doc?"

"Good. I like it a lot better than I thought I would," he said, tasting the rich dessert. The cake was moist and lightly sweet and the sour cream icing had just the right amount of tang. "How about you?"

"I was born here," Sheriff Miller said. "The only time I've been away was when I went to the police academy. Came back after graduation and haven't left since."

"Guess that means you intend to stay."

"Until the day I die. I could never go far anyway. My relatives are here."

"I never would have guessed you were Amish, Sheriff."

"Some people just aren't cut out for Amish life. I know I wasn't. I wanted to do something more exciting than slop hogs and clean stinking pig pens all day."

"Was it hard to leave?"

"For me, *nein.* For my parents, *ja.* My *daed* won't speak to me to this day." When he realized he'd slipped into *Deitsch,* the sheriff continued in English. "For the most part, Amish folks are willing to accept that some of us don't fit in where we were born. Bishop Harrison has tried to talk to my *daed.* But he won't budge."

"That's sad."

Sheriff Miller shrugged. "Nothing I can do to change his mind."

"Have you ever thought about going back?"

He went silent, and an odd look crossed the sheriff's face. Sadness. Regret. Perhaps a bit of both.

Having hit a raw nerve, Caleb suddenly felt self-conscious. It wasn't hard to guess Evan had a complicated relationship with his family and his heritage. He hoped the man would be able to reconcile with his parents before the rift became impossible to repair. Once people started passing away, the chance would be lost forever.

"I've no doubt in my mind Evan will rejoin the church someday," Levi said, pushing his empty plate away. "I didn't think I would. But once I came back to Burr Oak, I knew it's where I needed to be."

"You left?" Caleb asked.

Levi nodded. "*Ja*. When I was seventeen, I ran off to join the rodeo. Spent ten years chasing the circuit. Did my best to fit into the *Englisch* world, but it wasn't where I belonged. I was doing all the wrong things, and my life was a mess. Thankfully, *Gott* got ahold of me and gave me a good shake."

Intrigued, Caleb leaned forward. "Did you find it difficult returning to being Amish?"

"You mean, was it hard to give up my truck and things like that?" Brushing a few crumbs off his lap, Levi shook his head. "Not at all." He laughed. "It's not like we live in the dark ages. Most appliances are battery or propane-powered, so electricity isn't needed. If I can't take a horse and buggy, one of the hands can drive me. And we are allowed to use the internet and cell phones for business. The difference is we know these things are just tools. And like any tool, you put it down at the end of the day."

"That makes sense."

"It was a *gut* decision for Seth, too. He was six when we came back. He works hard as any man and can already rope and herd cattle. And he does his carvings. He's won prizes at the county fair and makes extra money selling them at the farmer's market."

"Gail isn't Seth's mother?"

Taking no offense, Levi shook his head. "Seth's mother was *Englisch*. She passed when Seth was about Sammy's age. After we got married, Gail claimed Seth as her *sohn* and you couldn't convince him otherwise now."

"Just for conversation, can someone who is not Amish join the church?"

"You wouldn't be thinking about it, would you, Doc?"

Caleb sat there, not sure how to respond. On one hand, he wanted to say yes. On the other, he didn't want to make a fool out of himself.

"I'm just curious if outsiders have ever converted."

"You'd have to ask the bishop," Levi volunteered. "A couple of *Englisch* fellows working on the ranch mentioned it a time or two. But that's just because they fell for an Amish girl and wanted to walk about with her. Usually, they give up the notion after a couple of months."

Sheriff Miller shook his head. "I've not known a seeker to stick with it yet."

"Seeker?"

"That's what we call folks who are curious about the Amish way of life," he explained. "Some even test Plain living for a while, but in the end decide it's not for them. Others choose to stay and enjoy living among the Plain folks. There are no wrong choices. Everyone's different."

Dessert finished, Caleb sipped his soft drink. "I suppose a person would have to show a certain amount of commitment to be taken seriously."

"*Ach*, that's for sure," Levi said. "I was born in the faith, and it wasn't easy for me."

Caleb lowered his cup. "I'd like to hear how you did it."

Levi leaned back in his chair. "Seeing as I was gone for so long, the first thing I had to do was declare my intent to come back to the church. It helped that Gail and her *schwestern* were willing to sponsor me."

"You needed a sponsor?"

Levi laughed in his good-natured way. "*Ja*. Once the bishop approved, I had to give up *Englisch* ways and begin living Amish. And once Bishop Harrison saw I'd recommitted myself to the Lord, I was allowed to begin classes to prepare for baptism. After I'd completed the *die Gma noch geh*—which means 'follow the church'— I had a meeting with the bishop to share my testimony of faith in Christ."

"The faith can be difficult to live by," Sheriff Miller added. "If an outsider wanted to try it, they'd have to attend church and participate in community events for an extended period. But Bishop Harrison is an openminded man and probably wouldn't deny someone just because they were born *Englisch*. He would counsel anyone who was willing to commit."

Caleb glanced between the two men. When he'd wrecked his SUV, he'd believed Burr Oak would be a place where he'd spend a day or two and then move on. He hadn't expected to be pulled into an emergency that would change his entire outlook on his past, his present, and yes, even his future.

The best time of his life—the happiest time—he'd ever had was that spent with Rebecca and her family. Their lives were simple. But that didn't mean they lacked the necessities that made living comfortable. It was quite the opposite. In a world driven by technology and distractions, the Amish had adapted and thrived while maintaining a life devoted to God, church and community.

I want to be a part of that.

His thoughts strayed back to Rebecca. Every time he closed his eyes, he saw her beautiful face and the loving way she gazed at Matthew. Without knowing it, she'd stolen his heart. He longed for her touch. Her smile. Her kiss.

Caleb closed his eyes. Soon, he would have to decide what path he wanted to follow. He'd made friends. He'd found the Lord. He'd met the love of his life. He didn't want to leave.

Still, he hesitated.

Did he belong in Burr Oak? Or had his lonely heart prodded him into believing something that wasn't true?

"Rebecca, I've never seen you looking so happy," Annie Fletz said. "You're glowing."

Cradling Matthew close, Rebecca smiled back. "I love having a *boppli* in my arms."

"No one knew what to think when word got around you'd taken in an infant," Arletta Hersch said.

She laughed. "I must admit, it was a surprise. But I'm glad I did. He's brought so much happiness into my life."

"I would have done the same thing if I had the chance," Rose Burke said. "My last *youngie* has flown the nest. It's been so hard getting used to a *haus* without *kinder.*" A short, round woman with graying hair and an infectious smile, she'd raised a large brood of nine.

"I'd love another," Annie said. "I've been trying to convince Herbert that we should have at least one more."

"The Lord hasn't blessed me and Oram yet," Arletta said with a sigh. "But we keep praying it will happen soon."

"How long will you have him?" Rose asked.

Gazing down at the infant, Rebecca shook her head. Knowing she would have to give him up was close to unbearable. It was a day she refused to think about.

"I don't know." She inhaled to clear away her anxiety. "All I can do is love him while he's with me."

"That be Mary Reese's *youngie*?" an elderly *Englisch* woman asked, speaking up for the first time. Dressed in black from head to foot, she'd occupied a chair near the group for most of the evening. One age-gnarled hand rested on the head of a cane. A young woman who accompanied her everywhere she went stood nearby, ready to help if needed.

Rebecca's brows rose. Apparently, Greta Melburn had an ear cocked toward the conversation. The widow of Hans Melburn, Greta had become a wealthy woman after he'd passed. Starting with just himself and a few hired hands, Hans had turned his little construction business into a large one, building and delivering custom sheds throughout the state. In addition to the business, Greta owned several commercial buildings in the downtown area.

Heart beating double time, Rebecca tightened her hold on Matthew. Dour and mirthless, Greta spent most of her time attending community events. It didn't matter what the occasion was. She sat on the sidelines and soaked up the gossip like a sponge. She knew everyone and nothing got past her.

"*Ja*. Mary is ill and unable to care for him."

"Shame, that is. Mary's *daed* used to work for my Hans." Blinking a time or two, she harrumphed. "All Donny Reese ever did was drink whiskey and drag that little girl around. Mary never had a chance after her mamma died. Shame she wasn't raised by her Plain kinfolks, but Donny clung to the bottle more than he did his faith."

Rebecca raised her brows. She had no idea Mary hailed from the Amish community, but it gave her hope for Matthew's future. Perhaps someday the young woman would choose to join the church and raise her *sohn* in the church.

"I don't know Mary's story. But I'm glad to keep her *boppli* until she's better."

Pursing her lips, the old lady nodded. "The Bible says he who pities the poor does the Lord's work."

"I'm trying. I plan to talk to the bishop about starting a *Boppli Bank* in the community center."

Greta's brows rose. *"Boppli Bank?"*

"A place where young *frauleins* like Mary can get supplies for their *youngies*." The more people who heard, the more Rebecca hoped they would want to help. "Diapers, clothes…things that will give them a hand up in caring for their *kinder*."

The old lady widened her eyes, showing a bright gaze. Despite her frail appearance, her mind was razor-sharp. "I admire your ambition. But it sounds like you're reaching above your means. It will take money to get the things you need."

Rebecca angled her chin. "I will supply the work and the Lord will provide what is needed for me to do it."

Stepping forward, Annie crossed her arms. "We all call ourselves saved and follow *Gott*. But if we do not serve the needy, then we deserve no salvation ourselves. You can be sure I will donate."

"I can certainly give some time and things *youngies* would need," Rose said and lifted her chin. "And so will my quilting circle."

"I'll donate, too," Arleta volunteered.

Annie waggled a finger. "I'd like to know what you'll do, Greta Melburn."

Returning an impassive look, the old woman was silent.

For a moment Rebecca felt pity for the old woman. Greta was nearing the end of her life and full of sorrow. Hans was gone. Both her *sohns* were worthless, never doing an honest day's work. Desperate to claim their inheritance, they circled like vultures over carrion.

"I expect nothing but your *gut* will, Greta. If you will add *youngies* like Matthew to your prayers, it would be appreciated."

Greta didn't blink. Slowly, her remote expression began to soften. The hand atop her cane trembled. "Do you believe you can do what you say?"

Rebecca strengthened her resolve. The idea any *youngie* should go without shook her to the core. *Kinder* were innocent and unknowing. It wasn't their fault their parents had made mistakes or were unprepared to cope with harsh realities. Someone had to step up, hold out a hand and say, *I will help.*

"I do."

Using the support of her cane, Greta rose. Discomfort creased her face, and the young woman standing nearby stepped forward. "May I help, ma'am?"

Arching her brows with disdain, Greta swatted the air. "Leave me be, child!" Slow, painful steps moved her forward at a snail's pace. Standing barely an inch over five feet, she was a tiny tower of determination. "I can see you have a heart for people and a heart for helping," she continued in her direct way. "If you believe you are up to the challenge, I will make you a pledge."

"Which is?"

"Whatever you raise in donations for your so-called *Boppli Bank*, I will double."

Rebecca's mouth dropped open. The offer was an answered prayer. "*Vielen dank*, Greta," she said, fighting to bring her pulse back to a normal level. "I am grateful."

"Don't be slobbering with gratitude," the old woman went on in her gruff way. "Once I make a deal, I stand by it. Call on me next week. I have a few ideas you might find useful."

"I will. *Danke*, Greta."

She turned and hobbled off toward the exit. Catching up, the young woman offered an arm. Mumbling under her breath and scowling, Greta allowed herself to be escorted out.

Everyone stared in her wake.

Annie clapped her hands. "Oh, Rebecca. How wonderful!"

Rose offered a quick hug. "*Gott* has truly blessed you."

"Greta Melburn knows everyone," Arleta babbled. "She will make sure word about the *Boppli Bank* gets out."

Excited by the commotion, Matthew began to wriggle in her arms. Opening his mouth wide, a loud cry burbled out.

"*Ach*, I think someone's getting cranky. We should go." Gazing around, Rebecca searched for a familiar face. She'd ridden with Caleb, and Matthew's car seat was in his van. But Caleb was nowhere nearby. Nor did she see any of her *familie* members. Most likely they were milling around in the parking lot, preparing to depart.

Bidding her friends good-night, Rebecca wove her way through the assemblage. Now that the desserts had been eaten and the games had been played, folks were ready to call an end to the evening. Several women cleaned up the dessert tables while the men put away tables and chairs.

"Rebecca?" A tall, angular man dressed in Amish clothing appeared out of the flock. A petite young woman dressed in a yellow dress, apron and *kapp* walked beside him. Her hand was hooked around his arm, indicating they were together.

Rebecca's eyes widened. Noel Yoast stood before her. She didn't know the woman who accompanied him. "I wasn't expecting to see you here."

Noel's nose wrinkled. "You know I don't like these things, but Sadie wanted to come," he said, speaking as if the presence of others was an affliction. Looking between them, he added, "I don't believe you've met my future *ehefrau*."

Heart dropping, Rebecca felt the floor sway beneath her feet. She'd heard the rumor Noel was seeing someone else but had paid the gossip no mind. "No, I haven't."

"Sadie's from the Oklahoma brethren. We will be announcing our intention to wed after Sunday's service."

She offered the girl a nod. Young, sweet and pretty as a spring daisy, Sadie couldn't have been a day over eighteen. "I wish you much happiness."

"Danke," he said, and eyed her back. "I've heard about your notion to open a daycare."

"I'm doing the work the Lord has led me to." Upset by the tension, Matthew squalled louder, attracting the attention of others. People began to stop and stare.

Noel made a tsking sound and raised a brow in disdain. "It is a shame becoming a *tagesmutter* to *Englisch kinder is the best you could manage for yourself."*

Rebecca stared in shock, wishing the ground would open and swallow her whole. Her tongue locked, leaving her unable to speak a single word.

"And she's doing an excellent job," a man's voice answered calmly. "God surely smiles on any woman who can love and care for a needy child."

Hackles up, Noel eyed the newcomer. "This must be the *Englisch* doctor everyone says you're walking about with."

"That's not true. Caleb is a *freund."*

Noel sneered. "There's no need to lie. People have seen you out together."

"All we've done is buy a Bible and drink a cup of coffee. If you're going to accuse us of more, maybe you'd better remember what the Lord says about bearing false witness," Caleb said quietly.

Indignation reddened Noel's cheeks. "I've no care what she does or who she does it with. She is not worthy to even care for a *youngie,* much less bear one herself. I've no doubt her sinful nature was the reason *Gott* struck her barren." Sniffing with disdain, he spun on his heel. Jerking Sadie after him, he stomped off.

The onlookers continued to gawk. A few pointed and whispered.

Rebecca began to tremble. Tears clouded her vision. Everyone in earshot now knew her secret shame.

I'm ruined...

Feeling the weight of their crushing stares, she rushed away. Somehow, she managed to make her way outside. Lost in the confusing jungle of vehicles and buggies, she stopped. Her tears undammed, sliding down her cheeks. A deep sob wracked her body.

"Rebecca!" Catching up with her, Caleb took Matthew out of her arms. Cradling the infant, he guided her toward his rental. He'd had the good sense to park beneath a streetlight by the corner curb, well away from the crowd. "Calm down. I've got him." He settled the infant into his car seat. "He's wet, that's all." Claiming the travel bag hooked on her shoulder, he changed Matthew with experienced hands. The infant's wails quieted.

Rebecca swiped at her eyes. "I'm sorry. I have no idea why Noel acted that way."

Discarding the used diaper, Caleb straightened. "Don't apologize for that jerk."

"In his mind, I'm damaged goods." Crossing her arms, she stared at the gravel beneath her feet. "Many Amish still believe it's *Gott*'s judgment against a woman who can't have *kinder*."

"I don't believe that's true."

She swiped at teary eyes. "Me neither."

"Then why are you crying?"

"Because now everyone knows." Her vision blurred

all over again. "I'm going to be alone for the rest of my life."

"No, you're not." Taking hold of her shoulders, Caleb's touch was gentle and firm. "If I could, I'd marry you tomorrow."

Shocked, Rebecca stared into his shadowed face His gaze collided with hers, revealing the depth of his feelings. The connection between them was real enough to reach out and touch.

Her lower lip trembled. "But you're not—"

Caleb caught her hands, cradling them between his. "I know what you're going to say, so don't. You're Amish and I'm *Englisch*. But that shouldn't matter. What counts is how we feel about each other." Caught in the moment, he pulled her closer. Dipping his head, his mouth captured hers.

It was wonderful.

And it ended all too soon.

Regaining her senses, Rebecca pulled away. Pressing a hand to her lips, she struggled to hold on to her fragile composure. What should have brought joy to her heart instead delivered a stab of agony. Only the fact she was baptized had kept her from admitting Caleb had gotten a grip on her emotions.

But she didn't dare say it out loud.

Committed to the Savior, she was expected to marry within her faith. If she were to leave, to choose love over the church, she'd lose everything she held dear. Bishop Harrison would have no choice but to place her under the *bann*. She'd be excommunicated.

A tremble passed through her.

How do I stop myself from loving the man I can't have?

Chapter Thirteen

The rest of the evening passed in a blur.

After her encounter with Caleb in the parking lot, they'd ridden home in silence. She wasn't sure what to say, so she'd said nothing. Using Matthew as an excuse to retire, Rebecca hurried into the nursery. Caring for the infant helped distract her from the emotions spinning through her. After getting Matthew settled, she'd dressed for bed. Kneeling, she said her nightly prayers.

Lord, if it's wrong for me to love Caleb, then I beg you—take these feelings away.

Slipping beneath the covers, she'd tried to sleep. But her restless mind gave her no peace. Near daybreak, she gave up trying to rest. The clock on the nightstand read ten after six. That would give her time to sit in the kitchen and have a cup of tea before the rest of the household woke. It would also give her time to think about what she wanted—no, needed—to say to Caleb. Stunned by his declaration, she hadn't known how to respond. She knew by the way he'd kissed her that his feelings were true.

But did she dare admit her own?

Belting her robe, she pushed her feet into a pair of slippers. Matthew slept soundly, giving her leave to tiptoe out. Leaving the door cracked, she stepped into the living room. Peering through the dim illumination, it surprised her to see she wasn't alone. A figure sat at the kitchen table. Bible open, Caleb's hands were clasped, and his head was down.

Rebecca stood, reluctant to interrupt. She'd also planned to spend some time with *Gott*'s word, searching the pages for the answers she sought.

A minute passed before Caleb raised his head. Hair mussed, a frown etched his lips, deepening the lines around his mouth. Mantled in solitude, he looked alone and forlorn. He motioned for her to join him. "I hope I didn't wake you."

Rebecca took a seat across from him, then folded her hands. "*Nein.* I had too many things on my mind."

"Me, too." Drawing a breath, he rushed out his next words. "I want to apologize for last night. I had no right to say what I did. I put you in a difficult position. I'm sorry."

Emotions knotting, she stared across the table. "You didn't do anything wrong," she admitted softly. "I feel the same way."

His frown faded, turning hopeful. "You do?"

"*Ja.*"

He slid his hand across the table. The tips of his fingers touched hers. "I hoped you would say that."

Rebecca welcomed his touch. A sense of comfort embraced her. The sensations of being loved and being in love made her head spin. Admitting her feelings out loud made her happier than she'd ever dreamed she could be. The truth was, she'd fallen for Caleb the first day they'd met. The amount of time they'd known each other didn't matter. She'd met the man she'd love forever.

She was happier than she'd ever dreamed she could be. But there were still problems. The path ahead wouldn't be easy. There was a reason *Englischers* were held at arm's length. Many, like Noel, wouldn't welcome an outsider.

Caleb's hand inched forward. His fingers traced hers, outlining each curve. "What do we do now?"

The intimacy of his touch curled through her veins. "We pray."

The sound of footsteps on the stairs warned them that others in the household were awake. Holding Sammy, Gail walked into the living room. Despite the early hour, she'd already dressed for the day. Her white apron was spotless. It wouldn't be much longer.

"You two are up early," she declared, entering the kitchen.

Unwilling to be caught in a compromising position, Rebecca pulled her hand away. The declaration of their feelings wasn't a decision that could be rushed. For them to pursue a relationship, Caleb would have to convert to her faith. That would mean a meeting with Bishop Harrison. To be accepted, Caleb must prove without a doubt that he was sincere in his desire to serve *Gott*. Anything less would be unacceptable.

Nevertheless, she couldn't help being excited about the possibilities. Promise seeded her heart, anticipating the chance to blossom into a bright future.

"I couldn't sleep," Caleb explained to fill the gap. "Rebecca was kind enough to keep me company."

"Oh? Something on your mind?" Ready to start

breakfast, Gail laid Sammy in his playpen. Eyes webbed with sleep, the toddler popped his thumb into his mouth and lay back down.

Tucking a bookmark between the pages, Caleb closed his Bible. "Nothing a little prayer won't handle."

"The Lord will always answer when we call," Gail said, sweeping cold ashes out of the belly of the stove before stoking it with fresh wood.

"That's what I'm hoping," he said, and winked across the table.

Heat crept into Rebecca's cheeks. She nervously folded her hands. "Can I help?"

Gail looked between them. A knowing smile lifted the corners of her mouth. "*Nein.* I've got it." Humming, she set to her morning tasks. Ten minutes later, she had a pot of coffee brewing. Throwing together the ingredients for a breakfast casserole, she slid the pan into the oven to bake. That done, she pressed out two dozen buttermilk biscuits from dough prepared the night before.

The smell of delicious food soon lured everyone downstairs. As always, the kitchen was a jumble of activity. Washed and dressed, the household prepared to greet the workday ahead. Florene volunteered to set the table while Amity poured coffee and set out condiments. Levi put Sammy in his high chair, helping the toddler spoon up oatmeal with a swirl of applesauce for flavor. Seth chattered about the new foals just days away from being birthed. Drawn into the good-natured banter, Caleb joined the conversation.

Rebecca smiled to herself. Though he hadn't been with them long, Caleb had managed to adapt to Amish ways without blinking an eye. It was only when he went to the clinic that he stepped back into the *Englisch* world.

A cry from the nursery shattered her thoughts. Awakened by the morning activity, Matthew released a hearty bellow.

Jumping up, Rebecca hurried to tend to him. Face red, his arms and legs beat the air. Scooping up the *youngie*, she carried him to his changing table. By now their routine was established. She knew the infant's likes and dislikes. He slept and ate well and responded to her voice and touch.

"Settle down," she soothed, tending to his needs with loving hands. "Once I change you, we'll be ready for breakfast." After his feeding, she planned to give him a sponge bath.

Done with the chore, she returned to the kitchen.

"*Ach*, look who is up." Pulling her casserole out of the oven, Gail set the hot pan on a rack to cool before sliding in the biscuits waiting to be baked. "I'll have food on the table in another ten minutes or so."

"I'll bet he's hungry," Amity declared behind a vivacious smile. "You sit down, and I'll make up his meal." Bustling to the counter, she retrieved a bottle from the battery-operated warmer before measuring his formula.

"*Danke,*" she replied, returning the smile. Amity was always first to volunteer when it came it helping with Matthew. She spoke often of the *kinder* she hoped to have someday. However, the Lord hadn't yet favored Amity with a steady beau. Nevertheless, Rebecca's younger *schwester* remained optimistic *Gott* would send "the right one" soon.

Taking her place at the table, Rebecca popped the bottle into Matthew's mouth. The infant suckled with enthusiasm.

Potholders in hand, Gail carried her casserole to the

table. The mix of eggs, chopped ham and hashed potatoes had been baked until firm. Topped with shredded cheddar cheese, the concoction was a gooey mass of pure deliciousness. A few minutes later, fluffy brown biscuits waited for thick smears of home-churned butter and a drizzle of golden honey harvested from the beehives.

Levi beamed at the food his wife delivered with a deft hand. "Looks delicious."

Done with his feeding, Rebecca pressed Matthew against her shoulder as everyone settled into their places. Releasing a healthy burp, he hiccupped before drifting back to sleep. Rocking him gently, she bowed her head for the prayer that preceded all meals.

"Amen," Levi finished, signaling that breakfast could begin.

Sliding a spatula into the casserole, Gail was about to serve up a heaping slice when a loud knock filled the air. "Whoever could that be?"

Levi rose. "Must be strangers. No one else uses the front entrance." Striding through the living room, he opened the door.

Sheriff Miller stood outside. An unfamiliar woman dressed in business attire accompanied him.

"Come in," Levi invited, showing the two inside.

Catching sight of the pair, Rebecca stiffened. Serious-faced and somber, the woman had pulled her black hair back in a severe bun. She was sharply featured, her mouth small and looked as if it had never once known a smile. Her glasses were fashionable, thin silver frames. Save for a slash of red lipstick, she wore no other makeup.

"Sorry to bother you folks so early," Sheriff Miller

said, removing his hat. "This is Bertha Howe. She's taking over Mary Reese's case."

Everyone nodded.

"Nice to meet you, Ms. Howe," Levi said. "We were just about to serve breakfast. Would you care to join us?"

Sheriff Miller shook his head. "Thanks for the offer, but we're pressed for time."

Bertha Howe's hawklike gaze zeroed in on the infant. "I assume this is the Reese baby?"

Rebecca nodded, rising from her place. Her legs trembled, threatening to crumble beneath her weight. "*Ja*. He didn't come with a name, so we've been calling him Matthew."

"His name is Benjamin," the caseworker said.

"Benjamin." She cleared her throat, attempting to summon her voice. "That is a *gut* name."

"I understand Benjamin has been under a physician's supervision while he's been here."

Caleb stood. "I'm Dr. Sutter," he said by way of an introduction. "The infant was born with a heart murmur. But it's not an issue. He's developing as expected."

"Then he'll be able to travel without complications?"

"As long as you take a break every few hours, there shouldn't be any issues."

Looking fretful, Amity wrung her hands. "Where is he going?"

"Benjamin is being returned to his mother," Sheriff Miller explained. "Mary's being released from the hospital. There are arrangements for her to live with a relative. I'm sorry, but I can't say where."

"I've spoken with her cousin several times," Bertha Howe added in her flat, nasal tone. "She's assured us Mary and her baby will have a place." Holding out her arms, she added, "I'll take him, if you don't mind."

Rebecca did mind. Nevertheless, she handed the infant over. As she did so, the ache of losing him settled in the pit of her stomach. It took every bit of her self-control not to break down. She'd known this day would come. She just hadn't expected it to arrive so abruptly. "We have some things we'd like to send with him," she said, forcing the words past the lump in her throat. "Would that be all right?"

Lips puckering with disapproval, Bertha Howe said, "I don't think—"

Sheriff Miller overruled her. "That's awfully generous. I'm sure Mary would appreciate having them."

Close to bawling, Amity covered her mouth with her hand. "I'll get them packed." Leaving the table, she hurried out of the kitchen.

"I'll help," Florene mumbled, looking miserable.

Gail swooped up her toddler in a protective embrace. "Me, too." Sensing something was terribly wrong, Sammy yowled and kicked all the way into the nursery.

Seth gazed at his empty plate. "I was just getting used to him," he mumbled.

Levi laid a hand on the youngster's shoulder and squeezed. "It's time for him to go be with his *mamm*."

"Guess so." Pushing his plate away, Seth rose. "I ain't hungry." Dragging his feet toward the back door, he claimed his hat. "I'd better go check on the horses."

"I'll go, too." Snagging his hat, Levi followed him.

Damming her tears, Rebecca forced herself not to cry. Despair stabbed deeply, twisting the blade with a cruel hand. Desperate for comfort, she looked toward Caleb. He was the last one left in the kitchen. Reclaiming his chair, he sat in silence. His expression flitted between sadness and resignation. Pushing out a sigh, he lowered his head.

No words were needed.

He was as devastated as she was.

On Saturday, the clinic was open from nine to noon. It was the last place Caleb wanted to be. But he'd promised Dr. Gordon that he would take care of his patients while he was recovering, and that's exactly what he intended to do.

Leaving Rebecca to go to work hadn't been easy. Shattered by Matthew's abrupt departure, she'd attempted to put on a brave face. But her watery eyes and quivering chin were a dead giveaway that her heart was breaking. She'd fallen in love with the infant, throwing herself into caring for him like a proud mother hen.

In the blink of an eye, Matthew—no, Benjamin—was gone. The baby was to be returned to his mother. That was the right thing to do.

Caleb's throat tightened. Benjamin would grow up knowing his kinfolks, knowing who he was in this world.

I still don't know my own story. The way things were going, he never would.

Did it matter? The past was in the past. Tomorrow was yet to come. The only time he had was now. Instead of dwelling on what he'd lost, it was time to focus on building the life he wanted. Today.

He scrubbed a hand over his chin. Since the day after he'd moved in, he'd stopped shaving. He'd never been attracted to the idea of facial hair, but now he found himself wondering what he'd look like with a beard. Those, he'd learned, were for married men. Though he'd seen bushy growths on older men, he'd noticed many younger fellows had theirs neatly trimmed to a decent length.

His thoughts all pointed down the same path. He wanted to stay in Burr Oak. He wanted to join the church and be baptized in the faith. Most of all, he wanted to court and, someday, marry Rebecca.

Spinning the fantasy in his mind was one thing. Making it happen was another. He had commitments in California to answer to. And he had no job in Texas.

A few phone calls will fix that...

Glancing at the clock, Caleb saw he still had a couple of minutes before the doors opened. Karyn had already come in to set up, as had the receptionist. He'd been told Saturdays were slow, which was why the clinic only stayed open half a day before closing. It didn't matter. He'd still be on call for emergencies.

He'd no more than put his hand on the phone when the receptionist poked her head in. "I hate to bother you, Doctor. Mayor Andrews is here. He's asked to see you."

He pulled his hand away from the receiver. "Oh? Send him in."

A minute later, a large man with a rolling gait walked in. "Dr. Sutter." Shutting the door behind him, he stuck out his hand. "I'm John Andrews."

Caleb stood to greet the newcomer. "Mayor," he greeted, returning the gesture. "What can I do for you?"

The tall man settled himself into a chair, wriggling to fit the narrow seat. "I know you're about to open, so I won't beat around the bush," he said, speaking in a forthright manner. "I'd like to offer you a job."

Caleb struggled not to grin like a fool. Pulling up to the clinic this morning, he'd taken a moment to pray about the matters on his mind. The biggest mistake men made was to run ahead of God. Proverbs warned that the heart might plan the way, but the Lord must establish the path to be taken. If Caleb intended to live by faith, he'd also have to learn obedience to the Holy Spirit.

Since his arrival, he could hardly deny his intention to start over in Los Angeles had been redirected. New people had come into his life. They had opened new doors. His priorities had also shifted. The big city no longer beckoned. Working in a cushy private practice that would allow him to swing a golf club and swill vodka tonics in a private lodge no longer appealed to him. Now that he'd experienced a life led to please the Lord, his spirit ached for the simplicity of home, hearth and a family to call his own.

Leaning forward, Caleb folded his arms atop the desk. "It's funny, but I can't say I'm surprised. Since my arrival, I've become aware of the problems the clinic is facing."

The mayor's expression darkened. "I'm afraid we've reached a dire crossroads."

"Given what I've heard about the state of Dr. Gordon's health, that makes sense. The fact that I am speaking with you and not him leads me to suspect he isn't going to be able to work much longer."

Andrews didn't blink. "I'm sorry to say it, but David Gordon is gravely ill."

"I see."

The mayor pressed his lips together. "There's no simple way to say it, so I will just spit it out. Dr. Gordon is in the beginning stages of dementia."

Caleb nodded. After speaking with Karyn, he'd begun

to suspect the same thing. Irritability, frequent mistakes and forgetfulness were just a few symptoms of the disease. Such lapses increased the risk of medical errors and the well-being of Dr. Gordon's patients.

"David's wife and I spoke about the matter. He's decided to take the next few months to transition into retirement."

"I agree with the decision."

"It will leave our town with no general practitioner," the mayor continued. "That's why I've stepped in. After meeting with the city council, I am happy to say we've approved additional funds to enlarge your salary." He looked across the desk, anticipation etched around his eyes and mouth. "I hope you will give it due consideration."

So, there it was.

Say yes and the job was his. Say yes and he could stay in Burr Oak. Say yes and...

A heavy hand struck the door, three hard fast knocks. Caleb jumped, startled by the interruption.

Without waiting for an answer, the door opened. Karyn peeked inside. Confusion mixed with frustration flitted across her face. "Dr. Sutter, there's a Dr. Wiley asking to see you." Gulping, she added in a rush, "He's the one Dr. Gordon hired. He's here. He showed up."

Caleb exchanged a mystified glance with the mayor. "Tell him to come in, please."

A man in his later twenties entered the office. Tanned and fit, he wore jeans, a T-shirt and sneakers. A mop of blond curls ruled over an infectious grin. "This is where I'll be working." Looking around with expectation, he gave a quick thumbs-up. "Cool."

Caleb felt his heart drop to his feet. Thirty seconds

ago, it looked as if his plan to stay in Burr Oak had fallen neatly into place. Oh, his plans were falling, all right. And shattering like a glass striking concrete.

"I'm Dr. Sutter. Dr. Gordon's out for a few days. I'm seeing his patients in the interim."

The younger man casually threw out a hand. "Nice to meet you."

Eyeing him from head to foot, Karyn shot out a frown. "You were supposed to be here on the fifth. Where were you?"

The newcomer gave her an odd look. "No. I'm pretty sure the twenty-fifth is the date."

Karyn's expression sagged. "He told you the twenty-fifth?"

Dr. Wiley's head bobbed. "Yeah. I have it in writing." Seeking to exonerate himself, he added, "It's in the letter he sent."

"Would you happen to have it?" Mayor Andrews asked.

Wiley dug a letter out of his bag. "Sure. Knock yourself out."

Opening the letter, Andrews scanned the page. "The twenty-fifth is what it says." Swiping a hand over his eyes, he read it a second time. "Well, this is certainly awkward."

Karyn bent over his shoulder to see for herself. "Dr. Gordon must have mixed up the dates." She nibbled her lower lip. "But we tried to call the number we had and got no reply."

"Where is it?" Caleb asked.

Karyn pointed toward an old-fashioned Rolodex. "There."

Caleb flipped to the *W*'s. Never one to use a cell

phone or computer, Dr. Gordon still relied on a manual typewriter for correspondence. All his contacts were typed and filed on index cards.

"Here."

Wiley checked the number. "That's not right. The last two digits are backward."

Caught in the grip of the brain fog brought on by his ailment, Dr. Gordon had most likely muddled the details. If nothing else, it proved that his illness was progressing to the point where it couldn't be ignored.

A question mark formed on Wiley's face. "Is there a problem?"

Folding the letter, Mayor Andrews returned it. "No. I assume Dr. Gordon believed you were qualified, or he wouldn't have offered you the position."

The sparkling grin returned. "I just completed a four-year residency in family medicine. I am an accredited GP."

Mayor Andrews's gaze shifted toward Caleb. "Qualified?" he mouthed.

Caleb nodded.

The mayor wasn't quite satisfied. "You're okay with the salary?"

A shrug rolled off the younger man's shoulders. "Sure. The money's fine. I don't need more than what's in my camper. Home is where it's parked."

"What about the location?" Andrews pressed, determined to present a deterrent. "This is a small town. And the Amish folks here are conservative. Not much for a young man to do."

Dr. Wiley didn't blink. "I was born in a town of about three hundred, tops. The only thing kids had to do was skateboard and study. I made a 4.0 GPA all the way through high school and college." Eyes narrowing, he gave all a suspicious look. "Am I missing something here? Don't tell me you hired someone else."

Feeling like an imposter, Caleb shook his head. "Not at all. The job *is* yours. Dr. Wiley."

Even as he spoke, disappointment stung its way through his chest. He'd been prepared to accept the mayor's offer. But it wouldn't be fair to steal it away from the man to whom it rightfully belonged. The only thing he could do was step aside with grace.

An icy sensation spread through him. The entire day had been filled with loss. Matthew was gone. So was the job he'd hoped to take. Having prayed on the matter, he realized the Lord had gently but firmly shut the door on his plans.

I wasn't meant to stay.

Chapter Fourteen

Pulling up to the ranch, Caleb felt a surge of conflicting emotions. This morning his future had overflowed with possibilities. Now, a black tunnel of nothingness stretched ahead. The setbacks morphed into demons, shredding and devouring his inner peace and joy. It felt like God was pushing him away. The idea he'd been deemed unworthy and cast aside twisted his stomach into knots.

His fingers tightened around the steering wheel. A sigh pressed through his lips. "You never belonged here, Caleb." Shaking his head, he slid out of the van. Roused from their naps, a couple of mongrel hounds loped up to greet him. He gave each dog a scratch behind the ears.

Throughout the day, everyone had chores to do. Working with the hired hands, Levi and Seth were in the corral saddle breaking a young horse. Florene tended her rabbits, changing the bedding in the hutches. A tame goat with a bell on its collar nibbled from a basket of vegetable culls meant for the hares. Gail worked in her garden, thinning the plants and gathering the produce that would later make its way to the dinner table. Her toddler played nearby, digging in the dirt with a toy shovel. Only Amity, at work at her shop in town, was missing.

Seeing him, Gail called to him, "Rebecca's over there."

Waving in acknowledgment, Caleb headed toward a grassy knoll near the bunkhouse. Taking advantage of the warm summer day, Rebecca worked over a basket piled high with laundry. Snagging a wet shirt, she gave it a brisk snap to take out the wrinkles before pinning it to the clothesline. As he drew closer, the clean scent of freshly washed clothes drifted through the air.

"How are you?"

Startled, she turned. Peering over the line, she offered a wan smile. Her eyes were swollen from crying. Shadows of sadness lingered in her gaze. She looked as miserable as he felt.

"I'm all right. Just missing the *boppli*."

"I miss him, too. He kind of wormed his way into everyone's hearts."

She snagged another shirt. Her hands shook as she pinned it to the line. "He needed to be with his *mamm*."

"It's always best. I hope Mary's able to get her life together and take care of him properly."

"They will both be in my prayers."

"You did a great job with him," he said, seeking to lift her mood. "Maybe you should think about applying to become to become a foster parent."

Hands trembling, Rebecca struggled for composure. "I—I don't know if I could. I knew Matthew would only be with us for a little while. But I didn't think it would hurt so much to give him back." She drew a long breath. "I don't know if I'm strong enough to go through a loss like that again and again. It's something I would have to pray on."

He nodded. Watching Bertha Howe take the infant away had almost been more than he could handle.

"I understand."

Shaking her head, she forced a smile. "Tell me about your day. I didn't expect you back until after noon."

He shrugged. "Turns out I wasn't needed."

"But I thought Mayor Andrews—" Catching herself, she pressed a hand to her mouth. A flush of red spread across her pale cheeks.

Surprised, he gave her a long look. "Did you know what the mayor was planning?"

Her flush deepened. "*Ja.* The day Evan and I met with him, he told us Dr. Gordon had become too ill to keep working." As if feeling guilty for keeping the secret, she hurried to plead her case. "He asked us not to say anything until he'd spoken with you."

"Matter of fact, he did come by to see me this morning. We were discussing his offer when the physician Dr. Gordon hired showed up. Apparently, there was a mix-up in his date of arrival." Continuing, he filled in the details. "Dr. Wiley arrived expecting to have a job. I couldn't yank that out from under his feet."

"You were right to let him keep the position. It's only fair."

Caleb scrubbed a hand over his mouth. The cup of coffee he'd consumed on the way home curdled in his stomach. "I guess that puts me back to square one. Matthew's gone. There's a new doctor in town. I guess I don't have any reason to keep hanging around."

She stared at him across the line. Surprise lifted her brows. "You're leaving?"

The ache in his chest deepened. "Yeah."

Her expression tightened. "When?"

"Tomorrow morning."

Mouth twisting wryly, she gave a brief nod. Without giving him another look, she plucked a pair of jeans from the pile. Shaking out the wrinkles, she hung them up. "I need to finish my work."

Blowing out a breath, he spread his hands. "I know. It's sudden. But I'm not sure God ever intended for me to stay." Anger suddenly rose inside him. A rough laugh escaped. "Matter of fact, I'm not sure God even exists."

Rebecca froze. Face pale and drawn, her hands visibly trembled. "Please tell me you don't mean that."

Caleb frowned. Why had he said that? He wasn't sure. Dizzy and slightly nauseous, he fought to make sense of his jumbled thoughts. Frustrated, he ground a fist into the palm of his hand. "I can't say what I mean because I don't even know."

Comprehension dawned. Tipping back her head, her gaze searched his. "Caleb, were you sincere when you accepted the Lord? Or did you do it because you thought being a Christian would magically fix all your problems?"

A shiver coursed through him. He was overwhelmed. "I—I don't know. Being with you and your family... It felt like I'd come home. That I was among my own." Thinking back on the last few days, he replayed the precious moments they'd spent together: reading the Bible, caring for Matthew and often just sitting quietly enjoying each other's company. For a week, he had the perfect little family. And then it was gone in the blink of an eye. "But now everything's been yanked away. I'm on the outside again, looking in. And I'm all alone."

Her beautiful emerald green eyes clouded even as her lower lip began to tremble. "That's not true. The Lord has a place for you."

"I don't think it's here." Placing his hands on her shoulders, he drew her toward him. "Come with me. We could start over in California. I make a good living. You would want for nothing." The moment the words left his mouth he knew it was the wrong thing to say.

Dismay flitted across her face. "You know I can't. I'm baptized. My vow to *Gott* is absolute and unbreakable. And I could never be with a man who didn't love the Lord first."

His hands dropped, hanging limply at his sides. The intensity of his emotions had become painful. His head throbbed. His chest hurt. The air he breathed felt like sandpaper scouring his lungs. A chill seeped between them, deepening his misery.

"How do we make this work?"

Rebecca's lips stretched in a bleak smile. "We can't." Lifting a hand to her throat, she swallowed hard. "Only *Gott* can. And He has chosen not to bless our foolish desires."

"It doesn't seem right. I haven't forgotten what I said this morning…or what you said. That's real. I know you feel it as much do."

"I do." Quaking, she drew a visible breath. "And that's why I must let you go. As much as I love you, we can't be together." Her voice broke. She choked down a sob. "The Lord would never want me unequally yoked with a nonbeliever."

Caleb's throat swelled. The thought of leaving and never seeing her again shredded him. The way she spoke indicated she believed the divide between them was too wide to bridge. Aching with regret, he was reluctant to accept the truth that she might be right.

"I—I didn't mean what I said. About God. Or not believing. I believe. With all my heart. All I want is to marry you. Love you. But I'll never be allowed to because I wasn't born Amish."

Moisture rimmed her eyes. "You are a *gut* man." Slipping a hand into the pocket of her apron, she pulled out a handkerchief to dry tears. "And I believe your heart is sincere. But you haven't yet learned to surrender your will to the Lord."

Nodding, he swallowed hard. Despite everything, her belief was unshakable. She was willing to accept grief, to accept loss, because of the trust she had in Christ. He realized then that being born again didn't mean all his problems would be solved. Finding faith meant the Lord would lend a shoulder to lean on during days filled with strife and sorrow. He still would know pain. Disappointment. Loss. But he didn't have to let it destroy his spirit.

Shame burned him. "I've acted like a fool. Can you forgive me?"

Forgiveness simmered in her gaze. "You need not ask. I could never be angry with you."

Caleb looked at her with longing. He would have given anything to draw her into his arms, hold her tight and never let her go.

That's something we can never do. Friendship was all that would be allowed. But it was better than nothing. And it would give him a reason to stay in touch.

"Before I go, would you do something for me?"

"Of course."

The lump in his throat returned. "Promise me you'll write."

Chin quivering, she rewarded him with a nod. "I'd like that."

"I want to know everything you're doing. The daycare, your *Boppli Bank*. And I'll want to know when Gail's baby is born—" He gave her a hopeful look. "Anything you have to say, I want to read it."

"You'll do the same?"

He pulled a breath to steady himself. "Absolutely. I'll write the first moment I can."

Lifting a hand, she pressed her fingers against his cheek. "I know *Gott* has plans for you, Caleb Sutter. Something wonderful is going to happen. And when it does, you'll have no doubt as to the Lord's might and grace."

Touched by her sincerity and warmth, he forced a smile. But tightness still gripped his heart, twisting hard. "I'm going to pray you're right."

She cocked her head. "You might not believe it now, but broken souls can become blessed souls if you let *Gott* do the mending."

Too emotionally choked to speak, Caleb claimed her hand and pressed the tips of her fingers against his lips. One last kiss.

He had no idea where God was leading him. He didn't know what waited for him in California. But if that's truly where the Lord meant for him to go, then he would obey without question.

Caleb was gone.

Rising before dawn, he'd quietly packed his things and departed. There was no need to say goodbye. *Gott* had settled things between them, putting each in their place. He had gone back to his *Englisch* world. And she had remained in her Plain one.

Rebecca wasn't bitter. Though she'd dreamed of being with Caleb, the Lord hadn't seen fit to bless their plans for a future. Haunted by their past experiences, both were still incomplete in so many ways. They needed time. To pray. To grow. And to heal.

Sitting at the desk in her room, she fingered the crisp white pages of her favorite stationery. She'd always been fussy about her correspondence, choosing to use a fountain pen over an ink pen. She loved the way it transformed the experience of writing, flowing across the paper with smooth easy strokes.

What do I say? Where do I begin?

A tear escaped, trickling down her cheek. They'd agreed to write, to share their lives through letters. No calls or video chatting was allowed. To communicate, they'd have to sit down and commit their words to paper. They'd agreed it would give them a chance to get to know each other better without the temptation of earthy desires.

Gazing at the blank pages, Rebecca quietly laid them aside. The Lord hadn't exactly said *no* to their relationship. But he had said *not now*.

As there were no Amish communities around Los Angeles, Caleb had promised he would join one of the Mennonite churches when he got settled. A bit more open to people from other denominations, the Mennonites welcomed all. And converting from Mennonite to Amish also wasn't entirely an unknown occurrence. He also planned to seek out pastor to counsel and guide him in his growth as a believer. Most of all he wanted to be certain that *Gott* had truly called him.

Given a year or two to prove his commitment to the faith, there was a possibility Bishop Harrison would allow Caleb to convert.

Only time would tell.

In the meantime, she had to get on with the business of living. She still had plans to move to town and open a daycare. Greta had promised to help with funding her *Boppli Bank* and had asked her to call within the week. Others had agreed to donate, too. That would take time to organize. She still needed to speak with Bishop Harrison about using the community center a few days a week, too. Lastly, Gail was due to give birth in a few short months. She planned to be on hand to help with the new *kind*.

So much to do. She'd be busy from sunup to sundown.

None of it cheered her. Emptiness gnawed at her insides. Her heart felt damaged, deeply and irreparably ripped open. How she longed to feel Caleb's arms around her, pulling her into his strong embrace.

No!

She thrust the provocative images from her mind. She wouldn't think about his touch. Or the way he'd gently kissed her. The sweet moments she treasured had turned into torture.

Simmering with discontent, she reached for her Bible. She needed to calm down and get her mind together. It wasn't the Amish way to question the Lord's decisions. She must find a way to align her desires with *Gott*'s. The Lord had instructed His disciples on how to pray. *Thy will be done.* Praying for *Gott*'s will to be done meant subjugating her own will and impulses.

Moving the lamp closer, she opened the heavy book to the section she'd bookmarked. In honor of little Matthew, she'd been studying Matthew the Apostle. A sinner and imperfect, the Lord had seen fit to call him. Despite his position as a religious outsider, Christ had given him a prominent position within the Christian sect.

Leaning forward, Rebecca propped her elbows on the edges of her desk. Immersing herself in the pages, she read each passage with care. It took only minutes for her gaze to settle upon the twentieth verse. The words jumped off the page.

"If ye have faith…nothing shall be impossible."

Blinking, she read the lines a second time. As she did, a comfortable warmth mantled her chilled spirit.

"*Ach*. Blessed be the Lord."

The door opened behind her.

"Rebecca?"

Startled, she turned. Florene stood at the threshold. Her hair was still covered by her sleeping cap, and her brightly colored patchwork robe was belted around her waist.

"Amity said to tell you breakfast will be ready in a moment."

Rebecca glanced at the clock on her nightstand. Immersed in study, she hadn't noticed two hours had passed. Ascending with blazing strength, the sun spread its gift of light and warmth across the land. The shadows of night crept away, sent back into slumber until their time to rise would come again.

"I'll be ready in a minute." Closing her Bible, she tucked it into her desk.

Florene gave her a concerned look. "Everything okay?"

"*Ja.* Why do you ask?"

"It's just that… Well, the *haus* seems so empty with Matthew and Caleb gone. I kind of miss them."

Surprise lifted Rebecca's brows. As far as she knew, her younger sister hadn't liked either. "We knew they'd only be here a little while. Matthew needed to be with his *mamm.* And Caleb has a job in California. His life is there now."

Florene shook her head. "I was sure Caleb was going to stay. He fit right in. I've never met an *Englischer* who acted so Amish."

"I'm sure he will come and visit. Someday."

"I hope so." Florene offered a tentative smile. "He really helped me figure out things about Zane."

"I'm glad."

"Me, too. Come when you are ready," she said and pulled the door shut.

Running late, Rebecca hurried to dress before making her way down the hall to the bathroom she shared with Amity and Florene. Face washed and teeth brushed, she headed down for breakfast.

The hour before church was always a rush. Because Gail had to wrangle Levi, Seth and Sammy into decent clothes, breakfast was a catch-as-can affair. Amity, who could barely boil an egg, oversaw getting food on the table. Her coffee was scorched and undrinkable. She'd opted to try her version of French toast. Slicing day-old bread, she'd soaked the pieces in a mix of eggs and cream before dropping them onto a hot skillet to fry. Except she'd forgotten to add butter. The smell of burning goop soon filled the air. Instead of serving up golden slices ready to be drenched in warm maple syrup, all she'd produced was a burnt mess. Slices of fresh fruit and a wedge of cheddar were more palatable.

A half hour later, everyone piled into the buggy. Because so many in the community lived miles outside of town, it made more sense for the congregants to gather in a single location rather than try hosting services in their homes. Plain and unadorned, the church building had grown exponentially through the years to include a suite of rooms to host meetings, as well as an entire wing that served as the community center.

Based on the needs of the congregation, the additions had been sanctioned by Bishop Harrison. Wide and open with plenty of room for tables and chairs to be arranged, it also had a small kitchen for food preparation. Throughout the week there was always something going on, pot luck meals, game nights and frolics for the *youngies*. Matchmaking events for those of courting age were always well attended, as were bake sales and auctions.

As always, the church was packed full. Those who arrived in buggies parked around back, placing their horses under a wide awning to shield the animals from the elements. Others arrived in vans driven by *Englischers* who made their living shuttling Amish folks.

Bishop Harrison stood in the entryway. Shaking the men's hands, he offered the ladies a friendly word, thanking them for their attendance. As the ministers prepared to speak at the pulpit, deacons helped everyone find seats. The women who taught Sunday school gathered the *youngies*, ushering them into a spacious playroom. *Frauen* with *säuglinge* were given the option of sitting in the rear pews, which were easier to depart if a *boppli* turned fussy during the three-hour service.

Rebecca also chose to sit near the back. She'd not been seated more than a minute when a soft voice brushed her ears.

"May I sit?"

Rebecca glanced up. Beneath arched brows, a pair of gray eyes met hers. The color was so striking and so unusual that there was no mistaking where she'd seen them before.

She has Caleb's eyes!

Eager to get a closer look, she patted the bare space beside her. "*Ja.* Please."

The woman sat. *"Danke."*

Pulse thudding, Rebecca gave her a sideways glance. Draped in black from head to foot, the woman looked to be in her later fifties. Sorrow and hard times lined her face, but the resemblance was there. Her features were feminine; softer, older, but the same. Thin and angular, she looked as if she hadn't enjoyed a good meal in ages. The cut of her dress and *kapp* marked her as one of the Ely's Bluff Amish.

A thrill coursed through her. She wasn't the only one who'd noticed. The day he'd met Caleb, Bishop Harrison had also remarked his face seemed familiar. If anyone would know, he would.

Located outside Burr Oak, Ely's Bluff was barely a blink in the road. The village had a post office and a cemetery. A foreboding community, members had doubled down on living their lives in austerity. Because their number was so small, their bishop also served as the minister.

A man well into his eighties, Solomon Bueller had recently passed. In the interim, a few of the Ely's Bluff Amish sometimes attended services in Burr Oak. No one knew them well. Standoffish, they spoke only when necessary. A few times a month they traveled into town for supplies. Farmers all, they only bought items they couldn't grow or make themselves.

Bishop Harrison often traveled to Ely's Bluff to help the leaderless congregants settle disagreements and other community matters. As voting for a new church elder only took place during communion, no one would be selected to replace Bishop Bueller for quite a while.

Nodding to the stranger, Rebecca offered to share her hymnal. Written in both German and English, the *Ausbund* contained centuries-old songs passed down through generations.

The woman shook her head, declining to join the singing. Silent, she folded her hands in her lap. Eyes firmly fixed on the pulpit, she didn't move during the entire service.

Normally Rebecca enjoyed listening to the sermons and singing the songs. Distracted by the silence of her companion, she barely heard the lessons preached for the day. The closing prayers couldn't come fast enough.

Finally, the clock struck noon. As the last hymn faded, the congregation rose in preparation for the pot-luck meal that would soon be served.

Giving a curt nod, the woman stood. "*Danke* for allowing me to sit." Turning, she began to walk away.

Unwilling to let her go, Rebecca reached out, touching her arm. "Excuse me for saying so, but you look familiar. Do you, perhaps, have a *sohn*?"

The woman paled. "How do you know of him?" Gaze clouding with regret, her composure crumbled. She raised her hands to cover her face. "I told no one…"

Chapter Fifteen

Los Angeles, California

One month later...

The office was a configuration of modern furniture and paintings, all emphasizing space and light. Tables of glass and brass. Chairs upholstered in a durable material a shade lighter than the carpet. And mirrors. Lots of mirrors. In every direction he turned, there was one to reflect what he had become, mocking what he once had been.

Gritting his teeth, Caleb tried to keep his temper in check as he went through his appointments for the afternoon. Most of his clients were rich folks with no real ailments. Many believed their membership fee to the clinic entitled them to instruct the physicians what they needed to be prescribed. So far, almost every patient he'd seen had requested prescriptions for opioids or narcotics for sleep, anxiety or stress. None of them seemed stressed, anxious or in any actual pain. He was expected to write the prescriptions, no questions asked.

Caleb swallowed the bitter taste rising in his mouth. He'd allowed himself to be lured by the money, ease and prestige of the position. Concierge, or direct primary care, was supposed to allow physicians to practice the way they wanted. But the super wealthy were willing to pay a lot of money to have access to the prescription pad. Worse, many of his fellow physicians seemed to have fallen victim to the lure of the almighty dollar. The employee parking lot was crammed with expensive cars. And living in a home worth less than a couple of million dollars was considered slumming.

One month in and he was miserable. Everything about the move to LA felt wrong. It was hard to keep his eyes on the Lord when all his coworkers wanted to talk about was their next expensive purchase or the minor celebrity they'd partied with over the weekend.

It wasn't the kind of company he wanted to keep. Like drawing a moth to the flame, the bright lights of the big city proved to be scorching. The traffic was bumper to bumper. The smog annoyed his allergies. He missed the wide-open spaces of Texas.

Biting back a sigh, Caleb shoved aside his day planner. He was tempted to buzz the receptionist, cancel everything and walk out. Thankfully, his attorney had the foresight to add a ninety-day right-to-terminate clause to his contract. Sure, he'd lose some bonuses and other compensation, but he'd be free.

Free to do what?

Admit defeat. Pack up. Go home.

But he had no home. No place to go. Nor did he feel any kinship to the people he'd grown up with. After he'd ferreted out the truth, Richard and Audrey's blood relatives had made it clear he wasn't a Sutter by birth.

He'd be tolerated, but he'd never be welcome. Truly, the crux of the matter was the Sutters's large estate. No one in the family wanted the money to go to an outsider.

Wracked with indecision, he decided to do nothing. A glance at his watch revealed he still had forty minutes left in his lunch hour. Rather than go out, he'd opted to order a ham sandwich and soda from the cafeteria. Hardly nutritious but he wasn't hungry anyway.

Opening a drawer, he retrieved a yellow legal pad. Through the last few days, he'd been working on a letter to Rebecca. Unfortunately, the page was blank. Since his arrival, he'd written and mailed three. All he'd received in return was silence.

Her lack of response was deafening. He could accept that one letter might have been misdirected. Perhaps even two. But not three. Of course, he knew why she hadn't replied. Being a sensible woman, she'd kicked him to the curb.

Caleb didn't blame her. As a suitor, he had little to offer. Even if he did, the fact he wasn't Amish would always be a stumbling block. He wanted to convert to her faith but doubted Bishop Harrison would allow it. He was everything Plain folks frowned on; a wealthy, spoiled *Englischer.*

Disappointment twisted his heart. An ache of longing throbbed in his chest.

Frustrated, he tore out the page, wadded it up and tossed it into the trash. Why bother? It was time to figure out his future. He already knew he wouldn't be staying in his present position. He wanted to do something that made a difference. Like Rebecca was doing. Despite the setbacks she'd faced in starting a social center for women and children, she'd found a way to make her dream to serve her community work. Her grit and determination to succeed was an inspiration.

A verse she'd once shared during Bible study sprang to his mind.

Thy word is a lamp unto my feet, and a light unto my path.

Caleb knew what he needed to do. Leaning forward, he clasped his hands and lowered his head. Suddenly, the comm unit on his desk buzzed and a nasal voice came through. "Dr. Sutter, there are some, uh, people asking to see you."

Caleb jerked up straight. His next patient wasn't due for another half hour.

He hit the reply button. "Who is it?"

"He says his name is Jim Dyette. He has your car."

Caleb perked up. He'd arranged for the body shop to deliver his SUV before leaving Burr Oak. As he had no home base, he'd given the clinic's address.

"Send him in, please."

A moment later, the receptionist opened the door. But it wasn't the burly mechanic who entered. Two women came in. The younger woman was neat in her simple attire. The older woman was clad in a similar style, but her clothes were black from head to foot. Head down, her hands were laced protectively.

Caleb's eyes widened. Delight flooded him. "Rebecca? Is it really you?"

Nodding, she smiled. "*Ja.* It's *gut* to see you, Caleb."

"What— How did you get here?"

She laughed. "I knew Jim was going to deliver your vehicle when it was fixed. So, I asked him to give us a ride. He was kind enough to oblige."

"I thought I'd never hear from you again," he blurted. "I wrote, but you never answered."

"I got your letters. But I didn't want to write back until I knew for sure. Then, when I did, I thought it would be better to see you in person."

Looking at her with curiosity, Caleb felt his heart thud in his chest. "Knew what?"

Her grin widened. "I have someone I want you to meet." Gently touching her companion's arm, she drew the woman forward. "I'd like you to meet Sarah Bueller. Sarah, this is Caleb. I told you about him. Now you can see for yourself."

The woman slowly lifted her head. A striking gray gaze collided with his. Though thinner and deeply lined, her features were eerily familiar.

Caleb felt the hair on the back of his neck rise. Certain his eyes deceived him, he blinked. No, the woman's face was still the same. Observing her was almost like looking in a mirror. Tall and spare, she was so much like himself, yet in subtle ways not.

Disbelief lanced through him even as an immense and completely unfamiliar tenderness filled him. A single word tumbled out of his mouth before he could stop it.

"Mom?"

"I might as well tell you, I didn't believe it myself," Rebecca said, explaining the chance meeting for the third time. "But when Sarah sat next to me in church, I knew right away who she was."

Grinning from ear to ear, Caleb shook his head. "I still can't believe you found her."

Rebecca looked between *mutter* and *sohn*. Side by side, the resemblance was even more pronounced.

Her mind drifted back over the last month. It hadn't been easy to break through the wall of isolation the older woman had erected around herself. A solitary woman, it had taken several weeks of coaxing to gain her trust. As they'd become friends, Sarah finally had felt comfortable enough to share her tragic story. Riddled with guilt and heartbreak, she'd isolated herself from most human contact. Her only solace was the church and her deep love for the Lord.

As if in a daze, Sarah continued to stare at Caleb. Sitting beside her *sohn*, she clutched his hand between hers. Tears of happiness glistened in her eyes.

"I never thought I would see you again. Praise be to *Gott* for answering my prayers."

"I've been trying to find you," he said. "But the court wouldn't unseal my records. I had no idea where to look."

The older woman's mouth puckered. Regret deepened the lines around her eyes and mouth. "That was my doing."

"Why?"

Dropping her gaze, Sarah pursed her lips. "I never wanted you to know you came from a *mamm* who couldn't take proper care of you."

Tenderness swamped his eyes. "I could never be ashamed of you. You gave me life."

"*Aye*. And I wanted you to have a *gut* one. Better than you'd have in Ely's Bluff." More tears welled in her eyes.

Listening to the exchange, Rebecca felt her own throat swell with sympathy. From what she'd learned during their talks, Sarah Bueller's life in Ely's Bluff was one fraught with poverty and deprivation. While she was growing up on a few patchwork acres of farmland, her *daed* was a harsh and unforgiving man. As bishop, Solomon Bueller ruled his small congregation with an iron fist, tolerating no nonsense. When she'd come of age, he'd forbidden Sarah to enjoy her *rumspringa*. Barely seventeen and aching to take a bite of forbidden fruit, the girl had rebelled. A brief fling with an *Englisch* boy had ended in heartbreak. And an unexpected pregnancy.

As the Ely's Bluff Amish were firmly Old Order, the slightest hint of impropriety was strictly frowned on. Being unwed and carrying an *Englischer*'s baby wasn't acceptable. Especially for a bishop's *tochter*.

Desperate to conceal her condition, Sarah ran away from the small community. A bus ticket had gotten her to Fort Worth. With no money and no place to go, she'd found help through an organization for unwed mothers. Given shelter and safety, she was able to deliver her *boppli*. But she still had no way to support herself or her *kind*. Knowing her community wouldn't welcome her home with an illegitimate *youngie*, she'd made the ultimate sacrifice. Certain he would fare better in the *Englisch* world, she'd given her *sohn* up for adoption.

Telling no one, she'd returned to Ely's Bluff. But her deception hadn't freed her from the consequences of her choice. The lie had become her shackles, plunging her into a life of austerity and solitude. Living with only the barest necessities, she'd prayed unceasingly for *Gott* to end her burden of shame and remorse.

Speaking in a trembling voice, Sarah quietly filled in the details surrounding Caleb's birth. Her eyes glistened as she spoke. Tears stained her cheeks when parts of her story overwhelmed her emotions.

"I never wanted to let you go." Eyes downcast, the older woman's voice warbled with pain. "But my *familie* never would have accepted you if I took you home."

"Because I'm half-*Englisch*?"

"Ja." She shook her head sadly. "The *Leit* would have shunned me if anyone had known I had a *boppli* out of wedlock."

"My father… Who was he? Wasn't there anything he could have done?"

A smile tottered across her lips. "His name was Lucas. Lucas Jackson." She fell to silence, gaze growing soft with remembrance. "Maybe if he had known about you, our lives would have been different."

Confusion clouded Caleb's expression. "I don't understand."

Pulled into the narrative all over again, Rebecca's pulse raced. Knowing the heartbreaking answer, she held her breath. Tossing up a quick prayer, she hoped Caleb would be able to bear the answer.

"He never knew about you," Sarah answered. "A few days before I found out I was with child, Lucas wrecked his motorcycle. It was a big, fast machine.'" A shiver visibly coursed through her. "It scared me when he rode it. But he wouldn't give it up. He…didn't survive."

"Oh, no." Caleb pulled a hand across his mouth. "I'm so sorry."

Emotionally wrought, Sarah gulped a breath. "After that, I didn't know what to do. I wanted to stay at Ely's Bluff and raise you in the faith. But as bishop, my *daed* would never have given me any peace. It was better to keep you away from him." Shoulders sagging with relief, she fell to silence. The truth had finally been revealed.

Reminded of her heartbreak after losing Matthew, Rebecca's guts twisted. She couldn't begin to imagine how Sarah must have felt; giving up her *boppli* simply to satisfy her *daed*'s archaic and puritanical interpretation of Scripture.

As bishop, Solomon Bueller had twisted his small community into something ugly and obscene. The *Ordnung* he'd set into place allowed no deviation from Scripture as he interpreted it. Their church was silent. No singing was allowed, not even songs of praise or glory. Only absolute obedience. Rather than vote in a new man to serve the remote community, Bishop Harrison urged the Ely's Bluff congregants to rejoin the Burr Oak Amish.

Seeing *mutter* and *sohn* reunited, Rebecca was sure *Gott* had reached out to undo the damage Solomon Bueller inflicted on his *tochter* and *enkle*.

Caleb gave his mother a look that said he held no animosity. "Stop blaming yourself. You did what you felt was right."

Sarah shook her head. "I did everything wrong. I let my heart rule my head and you paid for my mistakes." Her grip tightened on his hands. "Can you ever forgive me?"

He shook his head. "There's nothing to forgive. Not now. Not ever."

Sarah's face beamed. "Rebecca told me all about you. It warms my heart you know the Lord."

Caleb glanced her way. "I wouldn't have found the Lord without Rebecca." His smile widening, enthusiasm laced his words. "Her family opened my eyes to

God's mercy. And His great power. I'm a believer, and I always will be."

Rebecca's pulse stalled. This was it. The moment she'd prayed for had finally arrived. "*Gott* knew all along."

As she spoke, peace smoothed Caleb's brow. His stormy gaze calmed.

"Amen," he said. "I'm going home."

Epilogue

A year later...

Listening to the last notes of the hymn fade into silence, Caleb closed his hymnal. He'd waited all morning for the liturgy to conclude. Not because she wanted the preaching to end, but because the most exciting part of an Amish service had arrived. Today, members of the community who'd pledged themselves to the church would be baptized. Dressed in plain clothes, he sat beside the other men waiting for the ceremony to begin.

Turning his head, he glanced toward Sarah Bueller. "Today is the day," he mouthed.

Sitting a few rows away, his *mamm* smiled back.

Caleb's heart swelled with pride. No longer locked in misery, his *mutter* had learned to laugh and smile again. Discarding her black garb, she dressed in cheerful colors that complemented her complexion. During the service, she'd sung the hymns in a melodic voice.

His gaze shifted. Dressed in her Sunday best, Rebecca sat primly in her place. Gail, Florene and Amity sat nearby. Levi and Seth sat across the aisle, on the men's side.

As he waited for his name to be called, his mind drifted back through the last year. *Gott* had showered him with so many blessings it was hard to keep track.

Moving back to Burr Oak and joining the Amish community wasn't the easiest path to walk. One just didn't march into the bishop's office and ask to be baptized. There was a process. Like any Amish person who'd left the community and then returned, he had to comply with a strict set of rules.

Thankfully, Levi Wyse had agreed to be his sponsor. This allowed Caleb to live and work in the Plain community. However, Bishop Harrison had refused to start baptism classes until six months had passed. Candidates were only considered two times a year. Once chosen, a minimum of eighteen weeks was required for Bible study and counseling. After completing his classes and declaring his statement of faith, the bishop had invited him to become a member.

Focusing his thoughts, Caleb returned his attention to the service. The names of those waiting to be baptized were called. One by one, men and women rose, prepared to commit their lives to Christ.

The last to be summoned, Caleb crossed the stage and knelt. Held in high German, the ritual progressed without a hitch.

"Welcome, my *sohn*," Bishop Harrison added and shook his hand afterward. "May your time here be filled with joy and contentment."

The ceremony ended. Relatives and friends rushed to congratulate the new members. Men shook hands. The women offered a kiss on the cheek.

Sifting through the crowd, Caleb joined his *mamm*.

She embraced him warmly. "I've dreamed of this day."

Caleb kissed her upturned cheek. "*Danke* for having the courage to bring me home."

Spending time with Sarah, getting to know her, was the highlight of his life. The best parts were when she shared stories of her youth—and his *vater*. Touchingly, she'd kept a few photographs of her sweetheart. The ageing, yellowed photos helped fill in the gaps. Dark haired with an infection grin, his *daed* was a handsome fellow.

He knew who he was, and where he belonged. Best of all, he knew exactly how he wanted to serve the Lord. To earn his living, he'd partnered with Dr. Wiley to expand the reach of the clinic. Trading his SUV for a cargo van, he'd outfitted it as a mobile medical unit. Hiring an *Englisch* driver, he restored the old-fashioned practice of making house calls. Adopting Dr. Gordon's philosophy, he accepted what people could afford to pay.

Mamm's eyes moistened. "I couldn't have done it without Rebecca's encouragement. She helped me break my silence and speak my truth."

"I'm glad she did."

She daubed at her eyes. "Now that you're baptized, you'll be expected to take an *ehefrau*."

He chuffed amiably. *"If you're hinting about grandchildren, it's not very subtle."*

"I suppose I am." Turning her head, she gazed toward Rebecca.

Caleb swallowed hard. Though he and Rebecca had walked out—commonly called "dating" in the *Englisch* world—they had agreed to make no plans. To keep things proper, they only saw each other in the company of friends and *familie*. Sticking to the no-phones rule, they often exchanged notes, sharing their deepest feelings in writing. He treasured her letters, tucking them in a special box. When he missed her company, he took them out to reread.

"I'd like to," he confessed. "But isn't it too soon?"

Mamm cocked her head in a knowing manner. "You love her, don't you?"

"*Ja*. I do. But we agreed to be just friends until I adjusted to Amish life. I wouldn't want her to think I was rushing into a relationship just because I got baptized."

"If you love her, ask her." Spoken in a firm tone, *Mamm*'s words gave no doubt the matter had been on her mind for quite a while.

Flushing hot, Caleb slipped a finger in his collar and tugged at the right material circling his neck. The space around him suddenly felt hot and stuffy.

"Now? Today?" He didn't want to come right out and say his thoughts had gone exactly the same way.

"Time's getting away," *Mamm* replied sagely. "Don't let the woman you love go with it."

Caleb didn't have time to reply.Levi ambled over and slapped him on the shoulder. "Now you really have to give up those *Englisch* habits. Too late to back out." Mature in his Sunday best, Seth offered a handshake. "Guess this means we call you *Doc Amish* now."

Caleb snorted. "Sounds *gut*. I like it."

"Your *Deitsch* was perfect," Gail said, cradling her infant. Delivered without complications, sweet little Jessica was the spitting image of her *mamm*. At ten months old, she was an adorable sprite. "I'd swear you'd spoken it all your life."

"You got through without a single mistake," Amity

enthused. Tightening her grip on her nephew's hand, she kept him close. Three-year old Sammy would soon be old enough to join the other *youngies* in Sunday school.

"I could do it, too," Florene said, fingering the folds of her apron. "Sometimes this Amish stuff isn't so bad."

Amity cocked a knowing brow. "You would do well to make peace with your heritage," she shot back. "Life on earth is short. Eternity is forever."

Levi grinned. "Amen to that."

Caleb looked around. The only one who hadn't yet come to speak to him was Rebecca. Sitting in the pews, she hadn't rose from her place as the others had. Eyes closed, she sat in quiet repose with her Bible in her lap. Her lips moved as she prayed silently.

A rush of elation filled him. His heart never failed to beat double-time when he gazed at her.

He hesitated, reluctant to disturb her. A thousand scenarios ran through his mind. Each one was worse than the one before. What if she laughed in his face? Or said no.

Sensing his turmoil, *Mamm* gave him a prod. "I never had a chance to be with the one I loved. You do. Don't let this moment pass. It will never come again."

Gathering his courage, Caleb squared his shoulders. "You're right." It was now, or never.

Easing through the crowd, he took a seat across from hers. To avoid distraction and for propriety's sake, men and women never sat on the same side in church.

He cleared his throat. "A penny for your thoughts."

Startled, she opened her eyes. "Caleb. I thought I saw you talking to Sarah."

Nodding, he tried not to stare. With her high cheekbones and a dusting of amber freckles across her nose,

Rebecca was a fine-looking woman. But her beauty was more than skin deep. She glowed with the kindness and goodness that filled her. A sense of serenity and peace surrounded her.

"I was. She's, um, happy."

"I know she's proud. You can't know what it means to her you chose the faith."

"She said as much. And a few other things that were on her mind." Shifting his weight, he attempted to find a comfortable spot on the hard bench. "Things about you, as a matter of fact."

Curiosity lifted her brows. "Oh?"

"*Mamm* told me I needed to say something to you. And she's right."

"I'm listening."

"*Danke* for bringing me to the Lord. And for giving me back my identity."

A smile brightened her gaze. "I knew the day we met *Gott* had a plan for you."

"You were right. He does. And I want you to be a part of that." Sucking in a breath, he added, "Don't know if you thought about it or not, but now you can."

"Can what?"

"Be my wife. I'm asking you. Now. Today."

Shock raced through her expression. Her lips moved soundlessly, but no words came out.

Caleb swallowed hard. No backing out now.

Glancing around the church, he shrugged helplessly. The entire congregation had gone silent. People had picked up on the moment and were listening with rapt attention.

Determined to do things right, he rose and stepped across the aisle. Kneeling in front of her, he reached for her hand. Lacing his fingers through hers, he pressed their palms together. "I mean it. If you'll have me, I intend to marry you."

Visibly shivering, her mouth twisted wryly. "You know, there's a chance I can't—"

Caleb hushed her. "Blood doesn't make a *boppli* yours. Love does. If we can't have our own, we'll adopt."

She returned a long, aching look. "But I'd want a *hausvoll*." Voice cracking, she paused in an attempt to regain her composure. "At least three or four. Maybe more."

Laughing, he nodded. "Then I guess we'd better set the date." Yearning for her acquiescence, he tightened his hold. "The sooner we're hitched, the sooner we can get started."

Rebecca's cheeks flushed. Her eyes reflected the conflict between her mind and her emotions.

A long minute passed. And then another. Anticipation from onlookers flowed around them.

"Well go on," someone cat-called from the pews. "Give the fella an answer."

The tension shattered. Everyone laughed.

Rebecca's blush deepened. "I—I don't know what to say. This is so unexpected."

"You could say yes and make me the happiest man alive."

She met his gaze with a tender look. "*Ja.* My answer is yes."

Even as the words tumbled from her lips, Caleb leaned forward and kissed her. At that moment he was complete. Whole.

"She's gonna marry me!" he called to onlookers.

A cheer filled the church. People clapped. A few even whistled. Weddings were always a happy occasion to be celebrated in the community. Standing nearby, his *mamm* gave a nod and a smile.

Pulling back, Rebecca pressed a soft hand against his cheek. Tears misted her eyes. "*Gott* has truly answered my prayers."

Too emotional to speak, Caleb nodded. The Lord had brought them together and nothing would convince him otherwise.

Sending up a silent prayer, he thanked his Maker for the accident had brought him to Burr Oak. The dusty little town was his home now. A home he would share with the woman who had healed his lonely heart.

Today was the first day of the rest of their lives. Hand in hand, they would walk into the future.

With hope.

With faith.

But most of all, with love.

* * * * *

Dear Reader,

Welcome back to Burr Oak, Texas. I know it's been a long wait, but it took a little time to get Rebecca's story together. I love writing about the Schroder sisters and I'd like to share the inspiration for this book.

Like most writers, I spend time on the internet doing research. One day I stumbled on a story about a woman who had given her son up for adoption. She discovered him again when she met a young man with a birthmark that was strangely familiar... He was the child she'd given up over twenty years ago.

Inspired by the heartwarming tale, I decided to add an Amish twist to it. Both Caleb and Rebecca are dealing with hurt and loss in their pasts. Both struggle with their faith. And both experience the healing power of our Lord and savior, Jesus Christ.

I hope you all enjoyed my twist on this true life event. If you're interested in forthcoming books, stop by and visit me at www.pameladesmondwright.com. Be sure and keep an eye out for my next "Texas Amish Brides" title. Amity's story will be coming soon from Love Inspired.

I love hearing from readers, so feel free to drop me a note! You can email me through my website, or message me through social media. And you can always find me at: PO Box 165, Texico, NM 88135.

Sending love and light,
Pamela Desmond Wright

HARLEQUIN PLUS

Try the best multimedia subscription service for romance readers like you!

Read, Watch and Play.

Experience the easiest way to get the romance content you crave.

Start your **FREE TRIAL** at
www.harlequinplus.com/freetrial.